Camilla Isley is an er

she

adve

She'

hoar

duh!

the

food

A k

play

want

but s

You

cami

on T

@ca

face

By The Same Author

Romantic Comedies

Standalones
I Wish for You
A Sudden Crush

First Comes Love Series
Love Connection
I Have Never

New Adult College Romance

Just Friends Series
Let's Be Just Friends
Friend Zone
My Best Friend's Boyfriend

I Have Never

(A Laugh Out Loud Romantic Comedy)

First Comes Love

Book 2

Camilla Isley

This is a work of fiction. Names, characters, businesses, places, events and incidents either are products of the author's imagination or are used fictitiously. Any resemblance to actual events or locales or persons, living or dead, is entirely coincidental.

Dedication

To charity volunteers, thank you.

One

Never Make a Scene

The day it all goes wrong starts as a more or less ordinary one. My fit watch startles me awake at dawn and, forty minutes later, notifies me I've run five miles through Central Park. A perfect six-minute-per-mile time.

Back at Gerard's apartment, he's still asleep. I peel off my sweaty clothes, take a quick shower, and wake Sleeping Boyfriend with a kiss and the aroma of French-pressed mocha.

"Morning, sleepy head," I say affectionately.

"What time is it?" he asks, still groggy.

"Six-thirty, time to go."

Gerard groans and shuffles out of bed. We eat breakfast in the kitchen listening to the morning news. Me wearing a towel, him in boxer shorts.

Fifteen minutes later, I brush crumbs off my lips and get up. "I'd better get going, big day ahead!"

"Oh, right. The announcement for the new junior editor is today."

"Yes, this morning."

"Nervous?"

"Positive," I say, showing more confidence than I feel.

"Listen, babe," Gerard says, jaw twitching. A sign he's worried. "Why don't we go out tonight to... mmm... celebrate?" He's being awkward. *Why is he so tense?* "I want to talk to you about something important."

Something important? Is Gerard finally going to propose? After three years together, it's about time.

I smile slyly. "Sure, dinner out sounds amazing."

1

P&P. Promotion and proposal all in one day. This is going to be the best day of my life.

"Now I really have to get ready for the office." I kiss Gerard's forehead. "Text me when you've made a reservation, yeah?"

He nods, and I waltz into his room to change. Many people hate their jobs, but I love mine. Well, not exactly the job I have—advertising—but the job I *could* have starting today. Junior Fashion Editor of Évoque Magazine, the top female media brand in the world. Marketing was just my way in—an editorial position has always been the end goal.

Unfortunately, almost everyone else working at Évoque shares this dream. But I still hope to beat the odds. Annabelle Visser, our Editor-in-Chief—yeah, the mean devil wearing Prada—more than hinted that sales numbers will have a weight in the decision. Since joining Évoque five years ago, I've worked like a slave to become the star of my department. So if not written in stone, my promotion has at least been stitched in silk.

On all fours, I retrieve my sleepover bag from under Gerard's bed. One of my chief rules in relationships is *don't move in without a ring*. So whenever I spend the night at Gerard's house, I bring the essentials and leave nothing behind. This duffle bag is like an extra limb.

I shove my dirty running gear in a separate tote bag, then change into the working clothes I brought over: a black leather pencil skirt and emerald blouse that makes my green eyes pop. To intensify the effect, I shadow my eyelids to get that smoky look. At the office, exceptionally prim grooming comes with the territory and is expected of every employee.

Makeup done, I pull my natural strawberry red hair up in an intentionally messy bun, put on a bold shade of red lipstick, and wink at my image.

I'm the picture of a young, successful woman ready to conquer the fashion world.

From Gerard's Park Avenue condo, I can walk to work. The weather's perfect, and the late spring breeze only adds to my good mood. I wear foldable flats up to the edge of Central Park and then switch gears: plastic ballerinas for gel-cushioned pumps. I never show myself in public without heels. Not since that time when I went to Six Flags in my twenties wearing sneakers, and an attendant asked to check my height before he allowed me on a ride. For the record, I was a good six inches above the minimum.

In front of my office's skyscraper, I pause for a second to admire the building. Working at Northwestern, the publishing powerhouse of Manhattan, always gives me a thrill of pride. This is the place everyone wants to be. The building itself screams luxury and power from every glass panel and metal joint.

Ahead of me, the automatic doors sweep open, a strong, cool draft tightening my pencil skirt against my legs. Even the air feels expensive. As usual, I'm the first one in. *Good.* I always enjoy working in the quiet hours of the morning.

I stuff my duffle bag out of sight under my desk and turn on my laptop.

Will HR call me? Or will it be my new boss? This is the first time I've been promoted to a different department, so I'm not sure if the procedure is similar to same-department promotions. In the past, my current boss always delivered the news, but since I'll no longer work for her…

My landline trills, jolting me out of my thoughts.

I inhale, exhale, and then answer. "Blair Walker, Évoque Magazine."

"Miss Walker, this is Emilia Peterson from Human Resources. Please come up to my office right away."

"Absolutely, I'll be there in two minutes."

Emilia is our Talent Manager Coordinator—and she wants to see *me*. With a cheek-aching smile on my face, I rush to the elevators.

One floor up, I knock on Emilia's door, my stomach knotting in anticipation.

A muffled voice comes from behind the panel wall. "Come in."

If voices could be described as lipstick shades, Emilia's would be a Chanel Rouge. Suave. Confident.

I step into the office. Emilia—tall, platinum blonde, and lethally thin—lifts her icy gaze from some papers and says, "Ah, Blair. Please close the door and sit down." She gestures at the white chair in front of her white desk. Cold blue eyes settle on me. "Would you like some water?"

More some champagne. "No, thanks. I'm good."

"Very well, let's get straight to it." She folds her hands and sighs. "As you know, the position of Junior Fashion Editor was extremely coveted…"

Was? Is it mine now? I can't wait for her to say it, but I politely let her continue with her perfunctory speech. I can wait a few more minutes before I ask about the pay rise and extra benefits.

"…the race was tight, and you were an honorable runner-up…"

I nod my approval before my thoughts screech to a halt. *Wait, what?* Isn't this the part where she congratulates me and assigns me a new corporate phone? I was really hoping to get the new iPhone.

"What do you mean runner-up?"

"I mean you were an outstanding candidate."

"But not the winner?" My voice isn't nearly as steady as I'd like it to be—it projects a 99cents lip balm at best, regardless of the actual shade I'm wearing.

"Unfortunately, no. You didn't get the position," Emilia confirms, never taking her eyes off me.

"Who?"

"It doesn't really matter—"

"It does matter. Annabelle herself said sales figures would count toward the final decision. My numbers are better than everybody else's!"

"Your numbers are good, but not the best."

"No other sales manager signed as many contracts as I did this past year. I've put in more overtime and weekends to make sure of that. No one beats my numbers."

"Someone did," Emilia insists, her tone severe.

"Who?" I ask again.

For the first time, the corporate witch lowers her gaze, a shadow of guilt crossing her face. "Aurora."

"Aurora?" I repeat. "But her figures are awful!"

Emilia looks at me again, impassible. "One of her long-standing clients increased their expenditure considerably... it tipped the balance in her favor." Again, I sense she's holding something back.

Comprehension hits me. "You mean her mother bought the editor position for her!"

Aurora's mother, Rebecca Vanderbilt, is an iconic fashion designer with the power of old and new money combined. I never stood a chance against that kind of firepower.

"I know it might seem unfair..."

Are my ears functioning? Is our dear Talent Manager Coordinator trying to deny the injustice?

"Because *it is* unfair," I say. "You're ignoring the best employee to promote the one with a pedigree."

Emilia's nostrils flare. "We're promoting the employee who brought the magazine the most business, regardless of how they got it."

No point in arguing further. It's clear the decision is irrevocable. Emilia's immaculate white desk blinds me as I fight the tears threatening to shed. I take a few moments to steady myself before asking, "Is that all, am I free to go?"

"I understand you want to get this over with. You'll see we've put together an extremely generous severance package..." Emilia switches to a brisk, down-to-business tone so quickly it dizzies me.

"Severance?" I repeat.

"Yes. This might seem like a setback at first, but I'm really doing you a favor here."

"A favor?" I sound like a talking parrot, only able to repeat the words I'm hearing.

"Yes. Advertising is not your field. You don't like marketing, and I don't know when there'll be another editorial position available."

"Why are you firing me?" I ask, still in disbelief.

"Motivation is an important aspect of your job, and you wouldn't be able to bring your best effort to the table after today."

"Is it just me, or are all the other applicants being fired as well?

"Some other senior advertisers are being let go. Of course, I can't disclose their names," she says without batting an eyelid. "As I said, motivation is key—"

"Meaning you can no longer dangle the carrot of an editor position in our faces to have us slave for you day after day.

6

What's next? Are you hiring college grads to string them along instead?"

"Your replacement does not concern you."

"Oh gosh, that's exactly what you're doing!" I nearly shriek. "Are you trying to run for worst employer of the year?" The words leave my mouth before I can swallow them back.

"No, Blair, we run a business. I thought you were sensible enough to know that. And honestly, I expected you to behave like a professional. If anything, this behavior just wiped away any regrets we might have had about not promoting you. Really, Blair. There's no need to make a scene."

Those last words slap me harder than if she'd actually hit me. Making petty scenes goes against my creed, against my list of dos and don'ts. The list that's helped to keep me focused on my life goals and out of trouble since I was a teenager. I carry it wherever I go; it's the secret to my success. Until now, anyway. With Emilia's words still ringing in my ears, I picture the number one item on the list: *never make a scene.*

That thought is enough to bring me back from blind rage to controlled fury. Emilia's right, I don't need to humiliate myself any further. I'm going to leave in a dignified way and my head held high.

I school my expression into one of neutrality as Emilia slides a brown envelope over her stupidly white desk and taps it. "In here you'll find all the info about our offer. Please review it. I'll be happy to answer any questions you might have."

I take the manila envelope without opening it.

"I'm sure you did the best you could," I say. No point in trying to negotiate a better deal. When you get the ax, Évoque Magazine gives you what they deem fair and not a cent more. "Is that all?"

"Yes. It's understandable if you want to leave before

everyone else gets in. A security officer will escort you back to your desk to collect your belongings and will take your security pass on the way out."

Security, seriously? Are they afraid I'll steal a Birkin on my way out?

"Very well. Goodbye, Emilia," I say in the most civil tone I can muster.

Outside the office, a guard is already waiting for me. With a deep breath, I prepare myself for the most humiliating fifteen minutes of my life.

***

"You didn't get the promotion." Gerard's mouth hangs open. "I really wanted you to get it."

Oh? When did he start caring so much about my *career?* Being a corporate lawyer, he always seems so focused on *his* job. But the concern in his eyes is genuine and so sweet.

"Me, too, honey." I take his hand across the restaurant table. "But I don't want to ruin our night brooding over my lost job." I spent the entire day crying, curled in a ball on my couch, and only the prospect of tonight kept me sane.

Gerard looks aghast. "I thought this would be the best day to tell you... that you'd be happy..."

He's worried my job's demise is going to ruin his proposal. "You can tell me anything," I reassure him. "It doesn't matter what happened at work. We can talk about whatever it is you wanted to discuss." *Or you could just give me the diamond ring and be done with it.* "I won't be sad, I promise."

Gerard frowns. "I'm afraid you will be."

"Be what?"

"Sad."

"Sad?" He has it all wrong. Wedding planning is exactly the

kind of distraction I need from the pile of CVs I'll have to send to find a new job. Right, let's focus on the half of my life still going according to plan. "Why would I be sad?"

"Blair." Gerard sighs. "I think we should take a break."

"A break?"

The talking parrot is making a comeback.

"Yeah, we should see other people."

"Other people?"

"Yes, I'm not sure we're compatible."

I blink. "After *three years?*"

He nods. "Yes, you'll agree w—"

I narrow my eyes at him. "Who is she?"

"S-she? There's no one else," Gerard stutters defensively.

"Is it Laura?"

After endless arguments about my "unwarranted" jealousy for his secretary, I'm not going to pull any punches.

Gerard shakes his head frantically. "No."

Still, he dares to deny it.

"You're lying," I hiss. "How long have you been screwing her?"

"It's not like that." His entire face turns red. "We're…"

"What? In love?" I scoff. "An affair with your secretary—*seriously?* You're such a cliché."

"Blair, lower your voice. People are staring."

I sweep the room with my eyes and, indeed, more than a couple of heads have turned our way.

"Am I embarrassing you, Gerard? Is that why you brought me to this nice restaurant to talk, so we'd be in a public space?"

"Blair, we can discuss our problems like the two civil adults we are. There's no need to make a scene."

No. Need. To. Make. A. Scene.

My head begins spinning, filled with a whirlwind of

memories. My mother admonishing me whenever I threw a tantrum: "Blair, a well-educated young woman should always behave properly. We don't make public scenes. That's not what we do."

I remember the speech my ballet instructor gave me when I didn't get the lead role in *The Swan Lake:* "Blair, real ballerinas take setbacks with their heads held high. They don't make scenes."

Emilia this morning. Gerard now.

The vortex stops on a clear image of the list's number one item: *never make a scene.*

It's all been for nothing. All the sacrifices I made. All the times I said, "No," to anything even remotely fun. All the lost opportunities… *to live* rather than just behave. The list, my secret recipe for success, is worthless. At twenty-nine, what do I have to show for it? Nothing. No job. No boyfriend. Everyone thinks they can walk all over good old Blair because she's too polite to say anything. *No more.*

Rage takes over. My fury bubbles up and I vomit years of repressed feelings and self-imposed restraints on Gerard. "*A scene?* You don't want me to make *a scene?*" I get up and throw my napkin on the table. "Well, guess what! You're out of luck."

"Blair, don't—"

"Why?" I scream. "So you can run to your office's side dish with a clean conscience?"

"Don't talk about Laura that way. I won't allow it!"

"Do you prefer boyfriend-stealing bitch?"

Everyone in the room is staring at us now.

Gerard's ears turn a deeper shade of red. "Blair, please sit down, you're embarrassing yourself."

"I've nothing to be embarrassed about," I yell. "I'm not a cheating, lying bastard! Ladies and gentlemen, please give a round of applause for Gerard Wakefield and his mistress, the secretary, Laura."

A server arrives at our table and stares at us, perplexed. "Spaghetti marinara?"

In a crazy impulse, I say, "Mine." I grab the plate and before I know what I'm doing, I tip it over Gerard's head. "How's this for a scene, Gerry dear?"

Gerard shoots to his feet, his head, face, and suit dripping marinara. "You crazy bitch!" he shouts, dabbing the sauce off his face with his napkin. "It's hot sauce. You could've blinded me. I'll sue you for this."

"Please do," I shout back. "But be prepared to fight me in court. I'm sure the managing partners at your firm will be thrilled to learn of your extracurricular activities with their employee. They'll fire you on the spot!"

That shuts him up. Gerard opens and closes his mouth like a gaping fish. To stare at his spaghetti marinara-covered head would almost be funny, if the situation wasn't so tragic.

With one last glare, I storm out of the restaurant. Utterly lost and with no idea where I'm going, I run outside into the night. Oh, it felt so good to let it all out. Gerard's spaghetti-splattered head flashes before my eyes again and I can't help but laugh. A crazy, hysterical, uncontrollable laugh. Not being in control is great. Not holding back is fantastic. I should've done it a long time ago. I should've done so many things. All my life, I've had it backward. I've spent years caged behind the bars of the list, never allowing myself a moment of fun. That's over. The list's regime ends now.

I fish the page out of its honorific pocket in my bag and do a quick scan of all the taboos there.

"You're a fraud," I accuse it. "You're a useless piece of nonsense."

Years spent always being good, always being in control, always working hard—and for what? I have nothing.

My first instinct is to tear the sorry piece of paper into a million pieces, but a more powerful, self-destructive impulse takes over. Tearing the list is not enough; I need to completely overthrow it! Each line, each forbiddance, each bit of life I've denied myself will be experienced, starting tonight!

I scan all the don'ts in search of something stupid and reckless. My eyes stop on a vicious-looking set of words. I nod. It's as good a start as any, and I can tackle it right away.

Two

Never Get Drunk

My entire body aches. Even the tips of my hair are in pain. Instead of blood, it feels like acid is pumping through my veins, and my lids have been replaced by sandpaper. *What's happening to me?*

I try to move. Easier thought than done. My muscles feel like Jell-O. I'm stuck lying on something soft, something that smells like a cold winter day: pine cones and rain. Slowly, I open my eyes. Daylight stabs my pupils, sending tendrils of pain through my brain. *Where am I?* In a bedroom, it seems. *Whose bedroom?* Ah, that's the question.

Panic gnaws at my stomach, followed by a flood of nausea. I turn to one side and spot a glass of water and a blister of Aleve on a nightstand. *A lifeline.* I pop two pills and drain the water before collapsing back on the bed.

Whose bed? Oh, crap… I'm in someone's bed, in my underwear, and I've absolutely no idea how I got here.

The last thing I remember is walking into a bar determined to tackle the next item on the list: *never get drunk.*

Ding-dong. Mr. Hangover, we meet at last… Not sure I like you. I close my eyes, hoping the Aleve will act quickly.

When I open them again, I've no clue how much time has passed—a minute or an hour—but at least I'm slightly better. Well enough to roll over and retrieve my discarded clothes from the floor. There's my bag, too, and I always carry a compact mirror. *Face damage assessment time.* Gingerly, I flip the little metallic lid open. I've got panda eyes, but it's nothing some makeup remover wipes can't fix. The cool touch of the damp cotton is heavenly on my heated skin as I scrub myself clean. The soothing moisture helps also with the headache, so much so that I don't stop until I've used up the entire packet of wipes.

With my head a little clearer, I search for my phone and unlock the screen. Eight fifteen in the morning. There's an unhealthy number of missed calls and messages waiting to be answered. *Later.* My temples are still pounding. I open the map app to check where in the world I am exactly. The little blue dot stops on Brooklyn Heights.

What the hell am I doing in Brooklyn? How did I get here? Whose house is this?

Time to find out.

Still sitting on the bed, I put on the silky turquoise dress I was wearing last night—perfect for a proposal, not so much for a morning-after commute from Brooklyn. There's nothing I can do about the hair, so I scrunch the red tangles in a messy-for-real bun and stand up.

The room spins. I blink several times to fight the dizziness and shake my legs until the dress's skirt slithers into place, reaching my knees. Shoes in one hand, bag in the other, I drag my feet to the door and tentatively exit the bedroom to enter... a cool loft. One of those with brick walls and modern furniture.

Feeling like a burglar, I slip my pumps on and shuffle into an open-space living room with floor-to-ceiling windows.

"Hello?" My voice sounds thick.

"Morning," someone says. A *male* someone. "I was starting to worry you were dead."

"I thought I was d—" My throat catches as a guy in jeans and a light blue shirt comes out from behind a pillar. He's so good-looking I literally can't talk. Rumpled dark hair on the longish side. Dark brown—almost black—eyes, a strong jaw covered in five o'clock shadow, and he's smiling at me. A little sexy

14

dimple on each cheek. My stomach flips.

Is it the smile or the hangover?

But the real question is, did I have sex with this hunk? Well, I woke up in his bed wearing only underwear. I hope we did it. And I hope he wants to do it again because I can't remember a thing and the guy is too handsome for me to leave, not remembering having sex with him.

Eeeeee, somebody please censor my brain. Never in my life would I have had sex with someone I just met—but that was the whole point of throwing out the list and getting crazy drunk. If this man is the first outcome of my new lifestyle, high five to me. But how embarrassing not to remember if we slept together. What do I do? Do I ask him? I don't even know his name!

"Er, Blair?" he says. "Are you all right?"

Mr. Hot knows my name. "Yeah, super… mmm… uh…"

"Richard." He smiles again. "The name's Richard Stratton. I made coffee, you want some?"

If he wasn't already hot enough, the dude has an impossibly sexy British accent that's making my knees wobble. Either the accent or serious dehydration.

"Richard, sure." I pretend like he needn't have told me his name. "Coffee would be great, thanks." I stroll to the kitchen bar, sit on a stool, and drop my bag to the floor.

"Black? Sugar? Milk?"

"Sugar equals poison," I declare. "Do you happen to have almond milk?"

Richard's eyes widen.

"Black's fine," I hurry to say.

Mr. Hot hands me a mug. "You didn't seem to have a problem with the sugar rim of your cocktails last night."

"About that…" I take a sip of coffee, hoping caffeine will help my synapses connect. "I'm not exactly sure what… er. To be honest, last night's a bit—uh—foggy. How did we meet?"

"I called you."

"You called me?"

I have to kill the parrot possessing me and stop repeating whatever people say.

"Mm-hmm."

"How? Did I give you my number?" I think I'd remember giving my number to someone as hot as him.

"No, I got it through a friend of mine."

I frown. "A friend?"

The parrot lives.

"Yes, I'm the Editor-in-Chief of an up and coming web-based magazine. We're looking for a Fashion Editor—"

I hear magazine, I hear fashion, and the other shoe drops. *He's gay.* Ninety-five percent of Évoque male employees are gay. "Oh, you're gay," I interrupt him, a bit crestfallen. "Of course you're gay. That face is too handsome for you to be straight. I mean between the hair, the eyes, and the smile you'd have to go around with an I'm-too-hot warning sticker on your chest..." I'm babbling and Richard's eyebrows have shot up. *Blair, shut up.* But I'm possessed, and can't stop talking. "And that accent! Imagine what it would do to women. You sound like Prince William. Well, at least now I don't have to ask you if we slept together last night..." I brush my hand over my forehead in a gesture of relief and laugh nervously. "Phew."

Richard stares at me dumbfounded for a few seconds before saying, "I thought I made it clear last night I wasn't gay." His tone is dead serious.

Something in my guts twists. "You mean we"—I point at my chest and then at his—"slept together?"

"No, we didn't. I was mocking you."

"But I woke up in your bed in my underwear."

"I left you in my room with your clothes *on*. You must've done the undressing."

"Oh, so you *are* gay."

"No, I'm not gay." He scoffs. "It's just that so-drunk-she-can't-remember-her-name doesn't do it for me."

I'm too mortified to speak, so I hide my red-beyond-control cheeks by staring at the floor.

"Last night," Richard continues, "I called you to talk about a job opportunity, and you told me to join you in a bar in downtown Manhattan. When I got there, you were already drunk and delirious about a list, spaghetti marinara, and someone's secretary…"

I'm feeling smaller and smaller. From under my lids, I dare a peek at Richard.

"When we left the bar, I tried to put you in a cab to get you home, but you weren't able to supply an address. So it was either leave you on the street or bring you back here."

"Oh, okay." I drop the empty coffee mug on the bar and get up. "Sorry for all the trouble I caused and thank you for… mmm…" *Giving me a bed to sleep in instead of the curb? Saving my life? Making me believe for five seconds that we had sex?* I go with, "For hosting me last night. I'll get out of your way now." I pick up my bag from the floor and… I've no idea where the exit is. "Where's the door?"

"This way." Richard leads me to the opposite side of the room and stops in front of a metal door striped with faux rust, or real rust, I'm not sure. Cool, design rust in any case. "About that job interview," he adds. "You want to reschedule?"

"You still want to interview me?"

"You look suspicious."

Not look, am. "I don't mean to be rude, but if you're still considering me for a job after last night's stunt and this morning's conversation, you must be desperate."

His jaw tightens. "I'm not desperate."

"So what's your magazine's circulation?" I challenge.

"It's an online-only editorial hub; we hardly have any circulation."

"You've no printed edition?"

"No."

"Alexa rank?"

Richard holds my gaze for a couple of seconds before answering, "In the lower thousands. But most of our traffic comes from in-app views, with no ad blocking, and we want it to stay that way."

"As I said, you're desperate."

"Well, from what I gathered last night, so are you."

Ouch. Below the belt, Richard. Way below the belt. What else did I tell him while I was drunk as a skunk? Probably better I don't remember.

"Listen." He rolls up the sleeves of his shirt, and I get distracted looking at his forearms. *He has really pretty forearms. Correction: he has really pretty everything.* "I don't claim to be Évoque Magazine, but I'm working on making something fresh. *Something better.* I've put together a great team, so before you snub us, why don't you hear me out?" Richard takes a business card out of his pocket and hands it over.

As he comes closer, I get a whiff of that same pine cones and rain scent I smelled in the bedroom. *His scent.* So, Richard was my cold winter day. The combination of shower gel or aftershave plus male skin is intoxicating. I bite the inside of my cheek to keep focused and take the card. "Thank you."

"Go home, take a shower, and come back to check us out at the address on the card. This afternoon, tomorrow morning. Whenever works." Before I can politely decline, he adds, "If nothing else, stop by so you can see my too-handsome face one more time," and winks.

My mouth hangs open, and my face sizzles in shame for the millionth time since I woke up. "You know you can't use anything I said while I thought you were gay against me."

"Nice try." Richard gives me a wicked smile and opens the door. "See you later?"

I scold him on the way out. "Maybe."

"This way."

He guides me down the hall in silence until we reach the elevators. There, I push the down arrow and wait. When the doors sweep open, I briskly step inside, push the lobby button, and say, "Goodbye."

Richard braces both arms against the doorframe. "I'll see you soon," he says, stepping backward, and, as the doors begin to move adds, "And I'll work on finding that sticker."

The doors close so that I'm left staring at my shocked, beet-red face reflected in the metal.

Three

Always Move Up the Ladder, Never Down

Phone in hand, I search for the nearest subway station to get back to my apartment in lower Manhattan. A cab would be much better, especially considering my pounding headache, but my recent unemployment status demands immediate cutbacks. I don't even have my foldable flats, so my walk of shame is painfully done on five-inch heels.

The ride on the crowded train, besides killing my feet, does nothing to improve my queasiness. I need to drink a gallon of water and run an hour to sweat out all the toxins in my body. But most of all, I need another coffee and a cool shower.

As I unlock the door to my apartment, the only positive thought I can muster is that, if nothing else, the list did produce one good outcome. Item number four, *don't move in without a ring*, saved me from having to sneak back to Gerard's place to retrieve any personal effects. The thought of him and his secretary doing it in his office makes my skin crawl.

Did he bring her home too? Did they do it in our bed?

Technically, his bed… but still. I suppress a gagging reflex and step into the living room.

"You're alive!" Nikki, my roommate and best friend, barrels into me as soon as I enter the apartment. "I was so worried." She hugs me. "And you're in one piece," Nikki whispers before pushing back. "You're alive and in one piece and now I can *kill you!*"

"Nikki, please," I plead. "I've had a horrible two days. Let me take a shower and then I'll explain everything."

"You didn't come home last night. You didn't answer any of

my calls. No text to say you were staying over at Gerard's either. So finally, I tried his number, and he yelled at me, saying you two were over. Then this morning I called Évoque, and some girl told me you were let go yesterday. I thought you'd jumped off the Brooklyn Bridge!"

"I didn't jump off, but apparently I crossed over. And, in my defense, I was unconscious most of the time I spent there."

"Unconscious? Were you mugged? Kidnapped?"

"No, relax. Nothing like that, I was only drunk."

Nikki crosses her arms over her chest, skeptical. "You're never drunk."

"I was last night. What are you doing home, anyway?"

Ten in the morning is too late even for Nikki to still be at home and not at least on her way to work.

"I have to catch a plane for New Orleans in a few hours, so no point in dropping by the office."

"How long will you be gone?" I have the scary feeling I'll need someone here to babysit me.

"Two days. We have to shoot a commercial." Nikki works in a digital media agency specialized in video commercials. "And I leave in an hour, so you have to spill the beans *now*."

"If you want to hear the whole story before I shower, I need coffee. Want some?"

"Sure."

We move into the kitchenette. Nikki watches me expectantly as I put the water on to boil, but I wait until after grinding the coffee to launch into my tale.

Nikki asks me a million concerned questions when I explain the circumstances of my breakup with Gerard.

"A plate of spaghetti over the head was the least he deserved," she says. "But are you sure you're okay?"

"Nikki, I don't know. It's only been twelve hours, of which

I can remember only three, four tops."

"So where did you spend the night? Did you get drunk and hook up with a random guy?"

"I wish. It's so much worse than that."

I tell her the rest of my misadventures as we wait for the coffee to steep in the French press.

By the time I reach my morning encounter with Mr. Hot, Nikki is laughing her head off. "You seriously told this Richard guy he should wear an I'm-too-hot sticker?"

"Unfortunately for my dignity, I did."

"So when are you seeing him again?"

I stop pouring the coffee. "Never!"

"Didn't Mr. Hot offer you a job?"

"Yeah, he did, at an 'online editorial hub.' Code for startup news digest with no traffic."

"What's the name of the website?"

"The dude gave me a business card." I fish it out of my bag. "Inceptor Magazine."

Nikki grabs her laptop and we look at the homepage.

"The graphics are cool, stylish even." Nikki scrolls through a few articles. "The writing doesn't seem too bad, either."

"'Not too bad' isn't good enough."

"What's the guy's full name?"

"Richard Stratton," I say.

Nikki types it in the browser's search box and Richard's LinkedIn profile pops up first.

"Well, he's definitely *not bad*. And you woke up in his bedroom! You should work for him; if it were me, I'd work under him anytime…" She waggles her eyebrows.

"Oh, stop it." I cover my face with my hands. "You've no idea how humiliating this morning was."

"Richard didn't seem to care."

"The guy's desperate. Nikki, my curriculum is here"—I place my right hand level with my nose—"and his online whatever is here." I move the hand to my navel.

"Didn't you say you wanted to overthrow the list completely?"

"I did. But what has this to do—"

"Can I see it?" Nikki interrupts.

She's one of the few friends ever to be trusted with knowledge of the list's existence.

"Why?"

"I want to check something."

I search for the slip of paper inside its honorary pocket in my bag, but it's not there. I rummage through the main compartment and find it crumpled at the bottom.

"Here." I hand it over.

Nikki snatches the list from me, gets hold of a pen, and searches the various items with her eyes. "So, we can cross out never make a scene and never get drunk." She draws two lines on the respective entries. "And here, number fifteen, always move up the ladder, never down." Nikki pins me with a satisfied stare. "You're so taking the job."

***

I wait until the next morning to crawl back to Brooklyn, buying myself some time to become human again. As awakenings go, today couldn't be any more different from yesterday. The fit watch goes off at five thirty a.m., and on autopilot I shuffle out bed, dress in sporty clothes, and go for a run. From my apartment, I jog up Canal St. to the Hudson River waterfront and then up to 57th Street and back. It takes me longer than my usual time, but the ten-mile run does wonders to detox my entire system and puts me in a positive mood. *Thank you, endorphins.*

After a long shower and a healthy breakfast, I get ready to make the trip to hell—*er*, Brooklyn.

I walk to Canal St. subway station in my foldable flats and I'm about to automatically jump on the uptown train when I remember my real destination. My chest contracts in pain as I break out of auto-pilot and steer away from the uptown train at the last moment. I already miss Évoque so much, and not just for its geography and wardrobe perks. I miss the halo of power.

On edge before even starting the trip, I study the map to figure out the most convenient route to Richard's office. Irony of ironies, I still have to take the blue line. Only instead of heading up to Columbus Circle, I'm literally moving down and out of Manhattan to High Street, Brooklyn.

The address on the card brings me to one of those historic factory loft buildings. There's no reception so I walk straight to the elevators—not even proper ones, freight. Richard's card says third floor. I push three and wait for the freight machine to make its slow, slow way up. As I pass the second floor, voices drift down from above—raised voices.

"I'm having your license revoked," a woman is shouting. "According to New York MHY 33.21 in providing outpatient mental health services to a minor, the important role of the parents or guardians shall be recognized. That's me."

"Instead of worrying about having my license revoked," a man replies, "you should ask yourself why your daughter came to seek my help. And while you're at it, have a good look in the mirror."

"You've no idea the amount of trouble you'll find yourself if you don't stop meddling in my daughter's affairs."

"Well, someone has to deal with her problems since you clearly don't! All Tegan needs is for someone to listen to her."

Just as I reach the third floor, a door slams shut followed by a twin sound a few seconds later. Wary, I step on the landing. It's empty except for a girl braced against a set of industrial metal and glass doors. She's an Archie Panjabi lookalike in her mid-twenties.

"Don't mind our neighbors," she tells me. "They bicker all the time. Personally, I think it's only foreplay. Are you here to see one of them or one of us?"

There's a plate next to the metal doors saying Inceptor Magazine. I swallow; I've walked into a madhouse. "Hi, I'm Blair Walker," I say, extending a hand. "I sort of have an appointment with Richard Stratton for a job interview."

"Ah, Blair, I'm Indira." She shakes my hand. "The boss told me you might stop by. He's on a call right now, but I'm to give you the tour. Come in."

As I close the five-step distance between us, we give each other the ultimate once over. I take in her Brooklyn Soccer League pullover, skinny jeans, and black-and-white All Stars. Indira does the same with my below the knee dress and beaded sandals and it's as if we mutually acknowledge that we come from two different planets. Except her expression tells me I'm the alien in this zip code.

She guides me into an open-space office with oversized sunlit windows, exposed walls and beams, and wood flooring—straight from the twenties by the look of it. Someone would call it cool and modern; to me, it screams hipster.

"So." Indira points at a room with glass walls. "That's the boss's office."

Richard is sprawled out on a chair behind a giant black desk, talking on the phone. Seeing him is enough to make my throat clench.

Strangled, I only manage to hum an acknowledgment.

"Richard is our Editor-in-Chief, of course," Indira continues.

"All other editors are based here in this lovely open space, coexisting as one big, happy family."

I can't tell if she's being sarcastic or not.

"That's Hugo, the News Editor."

A guy with ginger hair and a short beard lifts his head and waves.

"Then there's Saffron. She's our social media and digital guru."

Indira points at a cute girl with long dark hair no older than twenty-two or twenty-three. Even their names are hipster-y, though Saffron's style is more grunge than bohemian.

"Zane is our Communications, Partnerships, and Distribution Manager."

Another bearded hippie waves.

"Ada is at entertainment."

A blonde girl out of a commercial from the fifties smiles and pushes her Cat-Eye glasses up her nose. I guess going vintage is equally accepted over here.

"And Nico is in charge of business and politics." Indira lowers her voice, "Never pick an ideological argument with him. Even if you're right, he'll bore you to death before you can prove your point."

I nod. A glance at Nico's bow-tied neck is enough to send off pompous alarm bells in my brain. The guy is frowning so hard at his screen he doesn't even notice we're talking about him.

"Over there in the corner are our techies and I'm in charge of everything non-content related. I guess this leaves you with all the fun stuff. Ah, and yes, that's our meeting room." She points at another glass-walled room next to Richard's office where he's still on the phone.

"You can either pick this station." Indira knocks on the desk to her left. "Or the one beside mine. I'm the best neighbor you could wish for."

"Well," I stall. "I'm not even sure if I got the job yet." *Or if I want it.*

"If you want it, the job's yours." Indira smiles knowingly. "Best piece of advice I can give you to survive around here is"—once again, she looks me over—"dress more casually and don't fall for the boss." Her eyes throw a wistful glance at the office behind me. "He's damaged goods."

I give her a questioning look, and she leans in with a conspiratorial air. "Rumor has it someone pulled a real number on him a few years ago. The boss hasn't been in a serious relationship ever since. Real commitment-phobe."

"You mean he's single?" I blab before I can stop myself.

Indira raises an eyebrow at me, and I blush.

Smooth, Blair.

"I'd hardly call it being single." She's looking at me with too-perceptive eyes. "Richard dates a lot, but no gal sticks around for long."

"You know what happened to him?"

"The gossip is he was about to—" She halts mid-sentence.

"Blair." Richard's voice, coming from behind me, sends a chill down my spine. "You've made it. Did Indira give you the tour already?"

"Hi." I turn around and am once again hit by Richard's unchecked good looks. "Yeah, we just finished."

"Perfect. Want to come into my office to discuss the gory details?"

"Sure."

I follow him and blush as the first thought that pops into my head is that we won't be able to have sex on his desk—as per the glass walls. *Stop it, Blair. Even if he wasn't about to become your boss, Indira says he's damaged goods and commitment phobic. Huge no-nos.*

Unfortunately, following Richard means I have a good view of his rear in a pair of nicely fitting jeans. The sight erases any rational argument the sensible half of my brain tries to make. So I stare at the floor instead and try to think of gruesome, unsexy stuff. *Fanny packs, ugly Christmas sweaters, spiders, Gerard and his secretary doing it.*

I suppress a gagging reflex. The fact that Gerard's affair is causing me more disgust than heartbreak is another clear sign my priorities have been all wrong. As the perfect boyfriend on paper, Gerard ticked all the right boxes in another stupid list of requirements. Good upbringing, check. Good job, check. Good looks, check.

Pity none of the important ones checked out. Faithful, nope. Committed, nope. In love, nope. This last one goes both ways, to be fair. Was I really ready to marry a guy only because he met my stereotype of a *"good"* catch? To be stark honest, I was. Not once I questioned my love for him, because he was too perfect, too sensibly right for me to debate loving him. Oh, no… I was turning into my mother without realizing it.

I wince.

"Everything all right?" Richard asks.

I try to compose my features. "Yeah."

He keeps the door open for me and shows me inside the office.

Once we're both seated on opposite sides of his desk, he asks, "So, what do you think?"

I try to come up with a diplomatic answer. "I shuffled through your newsfeed yesterday. You have some cool pieces and a fresh perspective."

Richard leans back in his chair. "You have any questions?"

I brace myself. Before any shop talk, I need to clear the air and make sure he's going to take me seriously. "Actually, I think we should address a personal issue first."

He seems surprised, but waits patiently for me to elaborate.

"I wanted to apologize for what happened at your house yesterday and for the night before... it wasn't... I wasn't..."

Richard's lips twitch, but he keeps a straight face as he says, "Like it never happened. You had a rough day, and I shouldn't have called for an interview at ten in the evening. From now on, we can have a one-hundred percent professional relationship."

The speech is meant to be reassuring, but the girl within me—the one crushing on him—can't help being disappointed. Anyway, he's right. If I come to work here, I can't have a thing with the boss. Also, for the first time, I spot a hardness behind Richard's gaze I hadn't noticed before. A coldness that says, I'm not into any other kind of relationship.

"Good." I nod. "Now down to business, can you share your advertising and traffic data?"

"No. Unless you work here, those are confidential. But I can tell you traffic had a year-over-year growth of two hundred percent and advertising went up by one-hundred and fifty percent."

"Okay." Those numbers aren't too bad. "What would my editorial budget be?"

"Ah." Richard rolls his sleeves up, a habit, it seems, and rests his elbows on the desk. For a moment I'm distracted by prime forearms display. I never thought it was possible to have a thing for forearms, but Richard's are proving me wrong. I miss the first part of his speech. "...it's basically on a contribution base."

Those last two words are enough to leave me horror-stricken and to force my eyes away from Richard's arms. "Come again?"

Richard takes a deep breath; we both know this is a hard sell.

"In a nutshell, each editor's budget depends on how much advertising he or she can bring in."

I swallow. "Mhm, but since I'm starting a brand new section, you must have something set aside for me to build on."

"Unfortunately, no." Richard shakes his handsome head.

"Hold on. You seriously mean you want me to start from scratch? How am I supposed to attract advertisers with no published articles?"

"That's why I needed someone with the creative, editorial potential, but also with the marketing experience. I'm sure you made plenty of contacts while working at Évoque. There must be some fashion influencer or big beauty blogger you can get on board."

I wrinkle my nose; this last part stinks even more. "Wait, are you offering me a position as Fashion Editor or Beauty Editor?"

Richard blinks. "Isn't it the same thing?"

I sag in my chair, a tiny pain starting in my chest. "You expect me to run an entire women's magazine on my own, and with no budget?"

Richard's mouth twitches at the corners again. "You would have complete creative independence."

I grimace. "How wonderful."

He fixes those impossibly gorgeous mocha-brown eyes on me. "And you get to keep a five percent commission on all advertisements sold as part of your compensation package."

The tightening in my chest worsens. Am I having a panic attack? *Pay on commission* are ugly enough words to unleash a panicked reaction. "Which translates into you offering me an intern-base salary, am I right?"

"I'm afraid we won't be able to match your previous compensation." Richard takes out a bundle of papers from a drawer and inches it toward me. "This is our standard contract."

I stare at the small—in all senses—numbers printed on the white paper. Yep, exactly the amount of my first paycheck after college. The pressure in my chest increases and I begin to feel lightheaded.

"But as I said," Richard resumes his pitch, "you'd get complete freedom on what to publish and state-of-the-art tech support." The handsome bastard smiles at me, giving me time to digest the news.

What choice do I have? A college graduate's pay that just about covers my half of the rent and food is better than no salary at all. At least until I can find another job.

Or maybe I should wait and see what else is out there on the job market. After all, I was let go only two days ago. If I'm careful on what I spend, I could survive on my severance check for a couple of months. That's when two nasty little words invade my brain: *student loans.*

No, I can't afford a single day with no income. And I'd rather be homeless than ask my parents for help.

Feeling like a trapped animal, I stare at Richard and ask, "Where do I sign?"

Four

Never Believe Gossip

Offices have a distinct and constant background noise. Especially open-space offices. The clacking of other people's keyboards, the clicking, the shuffling of paper, and the hum of whispered conversations. The background clatter is there, *always*. So much so, that a sudden silence is deafening.

I jerk my head up from the computer screen. I was right—everyone has stopped working. All my colleagues' heads are turned in one direction. Their expressions range from shell-shocked to mildly interested to unadulterated worship—this last one seems to befall the male population in particular. I follow the stares to the main entrance where silhouetted against the threshold is none else than Saskia Landon.

I join the staring contest. *Saskia Landon?* She is *the* model of the moment. Fashion editors all over the globe would claw each other's eyes out to have her in a photo shoot. Designers have to book her two years in advance for a catwalk. And she topped Forbes World's Highest-paid Models list, bypassing the runner-up by over thirty million. Saskia is the top one percent of A-list celebrities. *What is she doing here?*

"Is that Saskia Landon?" I hiss at Indira. "Am I seeing right?"

"In the flesh."

"Do we have a photo shoot with her? How did we manage that? Why wasn't I informed? I'm the Fashion Editor!"

"Relax." Indira rolls her eyes. "The lady is not here to work."

"Why then?"

"I suspect she's the boss's date for the night."

"Saskia Landon going out with Richard? *Impossible!*"

"You'd be surprised how well-connected Richard is. How else do you think he managed to pull together this"—she uses her pen to point around the office—"in less than six months? And then make it cash positive after only one year in business."

I want to reply, *by underpaying over-qualified employees like myself*, but I refrain. Instead, I say, "Okay, Richard knows people. But Saskia is supposed to be dating actors, NFL stars, or billionaires. What is she doing with Richard?"

Indira sighs. "They don't make for a bad couple."

I follow Indira's hinting stare toward the door where Richard has appeared next to Saskia.

Unfortunately, Indira is right. Saskia is tall, but Richard is taller. Side by side, both wearing jeans and plain T-shirts, they look like a Calvin Klein ad. Sleek, glamorous, sexy. Worst of all, they do belong. Richard with his dashing smile, one-day stubble, and effortlessly cool vibe. Saskia with her long limbs, out-of-this-world face, and hair to die for.

As if hypnotized, I watch Richard guide Saskia out with a hand on her lower back. I wonder how that would feel.

Would Richard's hand be warm on my back? Would I feel it through the fabric of my shirt? Would it send electricity up my spine?

The answer is probably yes to all three.

"Does that mean the receptionist is gone?" I ask.

Richard was dating a hotel receptionist when I accepted the job three weeks ago.

"They never last," Indira replies. "I told you the boss is damaged goods."

"Yes, but you didn't tell me why."

Indira leans in closer, speaking in a hushed tone. "It's just gossip, but..." She looks around for a second as if to check if someone is eavesdropping.

I make a "give it to me" gesture. Sometimes Indira is a bit of a drama queen.

"Well, legend has it the boss was about to get married, and the bride did a runner on him."

I gasp. "No!"

"Mm-hmm."

"You mean he was engaged, and his fiancée broke it off before the wedding?"

"No, I mean he was at the altar *literally* getting married and the bride panicked or something and ran out mid-ceremony. I don't know the details."

I purse my lips, unconvinced. "Who told you this story?"

"Oh, you know how urban legends start. One knows the story, but somehow can't remember how, when, or who told it. It's just something everyone knows."

"You think it's true?"

"I've never met someone as commitment-phobic as Richard. True, it could be innate. But somehow, I don't think it is. It's like the boss is trying too hard to pretend he doesn't care. All that cynicism has to come from a scar somewhere in his past. One that runs deep. Plus, all his friends from London say he was a completely different person before he moved here."

"Different, how?"

"Just the opposite of how he is now. The perfect boyfriend who would plan the perfect date for his girlfriend. Romantic, ready to commit, to start a family. But now... I mean he's a great friend, boss, and businessman. But he would make a dreadful boyfriend."

"Don't you think he would change if he met the right woman?"

"Why?" Indira gives me her signature I-see-everything stare.

"Are you nominating yourself for the role?"

My cheeks heat up and I break eye contact. "No, not at all. I was just speculating."

"Maybe one day, who knows? But I'm sure whoever that woman will be, she'll have to sweat blood and tears before pinning Richard down. And as much of a piece of eye candy as the boss is, that's just too much work for me."

"Yeah, definitely," I say awkwardly. "Who would want that?"

***

I spend the night staring at the ceiling torn between two opposite instincts. The first, my growing forbidden crush for my boss; the other, my unchecked work ambition. Having Saskia Landon do a photo shoot for Inceptor Magazine would skyrocket my style page to fashion heaven. But the mere thought of asking Richard to intercede with his supermodel girlfriend-of-the-week makes my skin crawl. Would he ask her as they cuddled in bed?

Yuck!

Unable to sleep, I grab my tablet from the nightstand to indulge in my new favorite hobby: reading Richard's weekly column. As Editor-in-Chief, he spends most of his time supervising other people's work. But the boss has cut a small literary space for himself where every Monday he writes an editorial. Sometimes it's humorous, other times it's more serious. But every single time his writing is brilliant.

Each week, the first thing I do over breakfast is read the newest column. Forget the Monday Blues, it always puts me in a good mood. And on nights like this, when I don't have a book or something else to read, I like to go over older pieces and get lost in his musings. Can you fall in love with someone by reading their words?

Yes.

No.

Maybe?

Anyway, Richard couldn't just be a piece of eye candy. Oh, no. He had to be smart, witty, and inventive, too. The more time I spend with him, the harder it is not to fall under his spell. And the more I read his words, the more I feel this connection with him. As do all the other women who read the column, I'm sure. I scroll down to the comments, penned, as suspected, mainly by female users. Male readers appreciate his writing, too, but I bet women are prompted to leave a comment by the author headshot posted at the top of the page. Could a man this intelligent really be afraid of serious relationships?

This is stupid. Richard is my boss. He'd be off limits even without his baggage. Richard, left at the altar. Could it be true? How could any woman about to marry Richard leave him? The gal must've been crazy.

I get a mental picture of his handsome, chiseled face staring at the bride as she runs down the aisle away from him. The intelligent spark of his chestnut irises subdued as he lowers his gaze to the church's floor in defeat. The lovely crinkles he gets around the eyes when he smiles banished by sorrow. Forehead creased. Jaw tense.

Then he raises his face again, and the gentle, trusting man is gone. Features hardened, cheeks gaunt, and lips parted in that cynic, uncaring grin Richard uses to scorn the world. He's a man wearing a mask. He's the Richard I know.

***

In the end, ambition wins out over my silly crush for the boss. The next morning I find myself knocking on Richard's door as soon as he gets into the office.

He looks up and smiles. "Blair, come in."

"Hi," I stutter nervously, taking the chair in front of his desk.

"How can I help my star employee?"

"S-star employee?"

Richard frowns. "Nobody showed you the numbers?"

"Uh, no."

His entire face lights up, and my stupid belly flutters in response. I need to swallow mothballs and kill the love bug infestation. Richard shuffles some stacks of paper on his desk until he finds the folder he was looking for. "These are the first analytics from your pages; it's amazing what you were able to do in only three weeks."

To build some one-hundred backlist articles, I had to call in every favor anyone in the industry owed me, and now I'm all spent. That's why a big, Saskia-Landon break is what I need.

"These looks great." I grimace, staring at numbers that are a teensy fraction of what I used to pull at Évoque. "But we need something truly spectacular if we're hoping for a real breakthrough."

Richard shakes his head. "Even with numbers as good as these, I can't allot any extras to your section."

"Okay." I flash him a mischievous smile. "But you can intercede with your connections."

Richard frowns questioningly.

"Was that Saskia Landon you left with yesterday?" I cut to the chase.

Richard's eyes widen. "Yeah, Saskia is a good friend."

A good friend? As in *only* a friend?! *Please be specific, Richard, these things matter.* Friend or *girl*friend? I ignore the ramming questions in my head and ask, "As your *good friend*, would Saskia agree to do a photo shoot for us?"

"We can't afford her."

"Don't you worry about that. Deliver Saskia for two hours, and I can get any brand on the planet to pay her fee, the photographer's fee, and book a year's worth of advertisement with us as well. Fashion houses will fight each other to jump at the opportunity."

"And you can guarantee this?"

"One-hundred percent."

"All right," Richard finally agrees. "Saskia leaves New York in three days; can you pull it off with such short notice?"

"You tell me which two hours she has and I'll sort the rest." I stand up. "Do you think you can get her to agree?"

"I can try." Richard smiles dashingly and with a sinking heart, I realize he might not have to try too hard. "Anything else?"

"If she says yes, get me her manager's contact information. Before making a proposal I need to be sure she doesn't have any feud going on with a designer or a photographer."

"Feud?"

"A Kanye West vs. Taylor Swift sort of thing, know what I mean?"

Richard stares at me blankly. "No."

"It's probably better that way. Anyway, as soon as you have news, please let me know."

"Will do."

I walk back to my station and sit at my desk, not at all triumphant. As I pull names for potential sponsors and photographers, I try to shake off the image of Richard asking Saskia as they lie on rumpled sheets after hours of mind-blowing sex.

***

Saskia agrees to the shoot. Was it because Richard gave her the best seeing-to of her life? Or are they genuinely friends? I don't let myself care. Instead, I wire my brain to professional mode and, in record time, I whip together the photo shoot of the season.

Photographer: Adam Bell

Sponsor, clothes, and accessories: Angelika Black. In-house stylist (Mandy)

Location: Grunge rooftop in Brooklyn

View: Manhattan Skyline

Makeup artist: Hire two just in case. All unexpected events must be covered.

So it is that the following Saturday morning by six o'clock, I've already been working for three hours. The set had to be ready early to shoot Saskia in the flattering light of dawn.

Our star arrived at five. We went through the racks of clothes, together with the stylist from Angelika Black, and Saskia agreed to every single outfit. She's so irritably nice. Honestly, I'd hoped she'd turn out to be a diva to compensate for her perfect genetics. But no, Saskia Landon is professional to a T.

More than that, she's super kind to everyone and even cracks jokes with the staff. Why would Richard ever look at anyone else?

The boss didn't come to the shoot. The only other person from Inceptor Magazine here is Saffron, our social media expert. She wanted to take some edgy backstage pics to build our Instagram feed.

As I watch the photographer take one perfect shot after the other of the most beautiful woman on earth, my emotions swing wildly between editorial lust and primal female jealousy. The stylist, Mandy, has no reservations. She can't stop clapping and squealing as she watches the shots appear on the screen after every click of the camera.

By seven thirty, we have enough frames to build two editorials: one for spring and one for the fall. To get the most out of this opportunity, I asked Mandy to bring some items from next year's collection as well.

Adam clicks his camera one last time and looks at me with an interrogative frown.

I clap my hands and call, "It's a wrap, everyone."

The staff claps along. Saskia hugs Adam, Mandy, and me. *Bah, she even smells good.* Saskia would probably hug everyone else on set, but her PA herds her downstairs to get changed before moving on to their next commitment.

Saffron comes to stand next to me. "Cool stuff," she says, sliding pictures on her phone with a finger. "Exactly the edgy, young vibe we needed."

I bend my head closer to hers to peek at the screen. "These are amazing."

If Saffron managed to snap pictures like that with an iPhone, I can't wait to see Adam's final product. He and his assistants have already dismantled the set and are carrying away the last bits of equipment. Before Adam leaves, we agree he'll send me as much as he can by Monday.

When everyone else is gone, I do a check of both the makeshift dressing room downstairs and the rooftop to make sure we left nothing behind. Alone on the terrace, I rest my arms against the railing to look at my old office building across the

East River. My eyes travel all the way up to the thirty-eighth floor, to Évoque's windows. Manhattan might've chewed me up and spit me out in Brooklyn, but I'll be damned before I renounce my dream.

"You'll see," I promise the sunlit building. "I'll be back."

Five

Never Make Impulse Decisions

Monday at the office, I'm happily shuffling through all the amazing photos Adam sent me when my personal inbox flashes on the computer screen.

Transfixed, I stare at the sender's name and subject for a few seconds.

```
Date: Mon, May 1 at 9:18 AM
From: gerard.wakefield@aol.com
To: blair.walker@yahoo.com
Subject: Our Breakup
```

I haven't heard from the ex since spaghetti night. What does he want? Despite myself, my pulse quickens. I let the mouse hover over the subject line without actually opening the email. What will the text say? What do I want it to say? Do I want it to be a groveling apology and desperate plea for me to take him back? *Sure.* But why? Is it only pride or am I kidding myself thinking I could get over a three-year story in less than a month?

After some serious soul-searching, I'm ready to read what Gerard has to say. Yes, I want him to apologize for cheating on me with his secretary. But, no, I don't want Gerard back. Our breakup, however un-classy it was on both our parts, was the right call.

One click and the full message appears on the screen. With every passing line I read, bile swells in my throat, and by the end, I'm full of acid and anger. To think that for a second I even considered taking him back!

When I hit reply and start playing whack-a-mole with my

keyboard, Indira stops her work and turns to stare at me.

"What's the matter?" she asks. "If you keep batting the keys like that your fingertips will bruise."

"The matter," I hiss, whacking along, "is that I wasted the last three years of my life dating an imbecile—"

"Imbecile?" Indira arches her brows. "Are you classy even when you swear?"

I finish my reply and hit the send button with satisfied ferocity.

Indira studies me a little longer and says, "Repeat after me. My ex-boyfriend is a dickhead."

"Is that the best insult *you* can muster?"

"I agree, we can do better. How about—"

My phone rings, interrupting her.

"It's him," I say.

I press a button to silence the ringtone.

"Care to tell me what happened?"

"The *imbecile* sent me an email offering not to sue me for throwing a plate of spaghetti on his *dick-head* if I sign a confidentiality agreement about his affair. He basically wants me to sign a document that says it's okay for him to keep screwing his secretary."

"Mmm." Indira purses her lips. "And what did you reply?"

"I thanked him for providing written proof of his misconduct at work in case the senior partners at his firm needed it on paper. And I told him he can expect news from my lawyer as I'm the one suing him for emotional damages."

Indira makes a fist and swirls her arm in the air in circles. "Go, girl. Finally, the redhead in you comes out!"

When the phone rings again, I'm about to put it permanently to silent but Indira stops me.

"Let me handle him." She picks up the phone, frowning at

the caller ID. "Edward Cullen? What's his real name?"

I have this little habit of naming my contacts after book or movie characters, and I still haven't updated Gerard's to a more appropriate one.

"Right, I need to change that. Real name's Gerard."

"What a sorry-ass name. Surname?"

"Wakefield."

Indira makes a gagging face and answers. "Blair Walker's phone."

I can hear Gerard's voice even if the phone's not on speaker. "Hello, who is this?"

"Hello, Mr. Wakefield. This is Indira Singh, Miss Walker's attorney."

"She hired an attorney? What's the name of your firm? Is this for real?"

"Given the considerable amount of emotional distress you caused my client, Miss Walker intends to pursue legal action against you. We should probably thank you for sending a written confession of your immoral conduct, Mr. Wakefield. It couldn't have come at a better time."

"*Blair* is pressing charges against *me?* After what *she* did?" Gerard is yelling now. I imagine his face red and contorted with rage as he spits into the phone, "Should I remind you she's the one who threw a bowl of scorching pasta over my head? Are you out of your mind? What kind of lawyer are y—"

"As I'm sure you're aware, I can't discuss any details of the proceedings with the counterpart. You can expect to hear from us soon. Have a good day." Indira ends the call and gives me the phone back. "Let the vermin squirm in fear for a little longer."

Our eyes meet, and we collapse in a fit of laughter. We stop, try to remain serious, only to burst out worse than before. It takes Richard passing by and asking us what's so funny for me to sober up. I give Indira a warning stare. I'd rather the boss didn't know I'm so lame my ex sent me a confidentiality agreement about his affair.

Indira shrugs. "Girl stuff."

I shrug as well, making an innocent face.

Richard shakes his head and moves along. "I suppose I don't want to know."

"Sage, boss," Indira calls after him.

We share another secretive smile and get back to our respective jobs.

Since my center of gravity shifted to Brooklyn, this is the first time I'm glad for the forced change of scenery.

I can't help but think my old colleagues would've been more snickering than supportive about my breakup with Gerard. Everything at Évoque was so competitive. All people thought about was who had the best job, clothes, boyfriend, house, vacations. No one would've had my back the way Indira did today. The bitches would've probably been happy my perfect lawyer boyfriend had ditched me. At Inceptor, I feel part of a family.

***

When the first editorial photo shoot of Saskia goes live, it's an instant hit. In its first week, it gathers so many page views that I'm sure I'll be able to pay rent this month. That five-percent commission didn't turn out to be so bad after all. Anyway, one success—however big—doesn't mean I can rest on my laurels.

"Do we have the budget to rent a car?" I ask Indira.

"Honey"—she detaches her gaze from her screen to fix me with a look—"after your Saskia Landon stunt, you can ask for a Ferrari."

"Thanks, but a compact for the day is plenty."

"That will do, too. Where are you going?"

"Cherry Hill, New Jersey."

"What for?"

"I want to convince a big makeup house to sponsor a regular feature. I convinced Adam's wife—the photographer for Saskia's shoot—to video blog for us. She's a YouTube tutorials star, and she's agreed to work with me. Now we're only missing some cool products for her to vlog about."

"When do you need the car?"

"Tomorrow. Please make the pickup time as early as possible and in Manhattan, near my house. The drive to New Jersey will take at least two hours."

"All right." Indira taps her keyboard. "You have a Hyundai Elantra booked for tomorrow morning at seven-thirty. Return time is the same the next day." She prints a page and gives it to me.

The rental office address is just a block from my house. "What time do they close in the evening?"

She checks the screen. "Six."

"Hopefully I'll be able to return it the same day. It would cost more to park the car overnight than to rent it."

"The joys of living in Manhattan," Indira replies.

***

As expected, the drive out of New York is a nightmare. But having left early, I manage to get to my before-lunch appointment in time. Brenda, my contact from my old job, welcomes me into her office with a tight smile.

Still, coming off from my Saskia Landon success, I'm confident. I finally have the validation my fashion pages needed. Now I need to secure the same big-brand recognition for the beauty section.

The meeting doesn't last long. Skeptical as Brenda might have been, I came with my marketing guns loaded. Having Tracy Bell as the beauty vlogger and mentioning Saskia is enough to lock in a weekly supply of products for Tracy to test, review, and give away. Brenda doesn't agree on any extra paid advertisement, but that was only a long shot I had to try. All in all, I get to go home satisfied.

When I stop to fill the tank two hours later, my body is a muscle-cramping mess. I just crossed over into Manhattan, and I can't wait to give this metal box back. I use every movement getting out of the car to stretch a needy muscle, anticipating the yoga workout I've been planning in my head for the entire return drive.

It takes me a minute to locate the button to release the gasoline cover. Why would they hide it almost under the driver seat? As I round the car, I catch the eye of a guy refueling his bike at the next pump. He's clearly giving me a sexist woman-at-the-wheel stare. Chin up, I ignore him and move along with my business.

As I'm struggling to lock the hose, something cold and moist touches my naked calf. I jerk back and yell in surprise. Unfortunately, I yank the hose away from the tank as well, spilling gasoline all over the station and my legs. I release the handle and try to assess the damage. My skirt is soaked and I've spilled gasoline on the side of the car and... on the dog at my feet.

"Hello. Who are you?"

The small animal yelps pityingly and sniffs my calf again. I put the hose back into the tank and kneel down. The dog, more of a puppy actually, tries to jump in my lap. "Oh, look at you. Are you alone?"

I get another cry for an answer. My heart breaks. The pup

looks like a golden retriever with more of a dirty brown fur and a longer snout. He must be a mutt. Apparently an abandoned mutt.

"You smell awful." He must have even before my gasoline shower seeing how dirty he is. I pat his head all the same and he waggles his tail happily in response. "Oh, I see what you're trying to do. Forget it; I can't have a pet." As if in protest, the dog sits on my feet. Is he trying to prevent me from leaving? Maybe the puppy isn't as abandoned as he looks. What if it the gasoline alone got him dirty? He might be lost. But he has no collar or tag.

Let's finish with the gas, and then I'll see.

When the tank is full, I go inside the convenience store to pay. Someone there may know whose dog he is. But as soon as I step a foot inside, the clerk says, "Hey, miss, you can't bring your dog in here."

Startled by the remark, I lower my gaze. The pup has followed me inside.

"This is not my dog. Actually, I wanted to ask you if you knew who he belonged to."

"Are you sure it ain't yours?" The man looks suspiciously at my feet where the puppy has stopped next to me, sitting down as if trained to do so.

"Yes. I was filling the tank, and he came out of nowhere."

"Well, if it ain't yours, I'll have to call pest control."

"Pest control? He's no pest he's just an abandoned puppy."

"Sorry, but I can't have no stray dogs in my station."

"I'm sure there's a better way to solve the problem."

"If you're so worried about the fur ball, why don't you take it?"

"I can't keep a dog."

This statement earns me a desperate, pleading howl from the

little mutt.

"What?" I lower my gaze to him again. "You speak English?"

I get a subdued bark as a reply.

"Listen, miss, if you ain't taking the dog, I'm calling pest control or animal control or whatever you like to call it."

"All right, all right," I say impulsively. "Tell me how much it is for the gas, and I'll deal with the puppy."

"Thirty-nine dollars."

I give him my card. "Wait. Do you sell garbage bags?"

"Third aisle behind you."

I grab an eighty pack of perfumed ones, pay, and exit. Mr. Mutt walks at my heel again.

Back to the car, I kneel down next to the puppy.

"Just to be clear, this is a temporary arrangement," I tell him. I swear the dog smiles at me. "There's no way I can keep you in my tiny Manhattan apartment. Understood?"

I get two enthusiastic barks back.

I open the trunk, remove the security shade cover, and line the inside and the rear of the backseats with garbage bags.

"All right." I pat the bumper twice. "Up."

Mr. Mutt gives me another excited bark and jumps in.

"Please be good while I figure out where to take you."

He starts whining again.

Since my skirt is still soaked in gasoline, I line the driver seat with another garbage bag and search for a dog shelter on my phone. There's one not too far from my apartment. I copy the address in the map app and pull out of the gas station.

Less than a mile from the shelter, blue and red lights appear in the rearview mirror. The police must be trying to pull someone over. I keep driving, being extra careful to avoid any infraction, but the flashing lights stay with me. I check the left lane for suspicious-looking cars, but it's empty.

Those flashing lights are making me irrationally nervous, so I turn right even if the navigator is telling me to go straight. But I'm out of luck, the police car turns right after me, and not just that, they flash their headlights twice and turn on the siren.

Crap, they were following *me*. I pull over and watch the side view mirror as a police officer ominously approaches.

Six

Never Break the Law/Get Arrested

"Good evening, officer," I say, using my most polite, law-abiding-citizen tone.

The cop looks serious in his dark uniform, bulletproof vest, and heavy boots.

"Evening, ma'am. Where are you coming from?"

"Cherry Hill, New Jersey. I was there for a business meeting."

"And where are you headed?"

"To Animal Heaven. I found a stray dog."

Mr. Mutt barks on cue.

The officer leans in closer to the window and his nostrils flare.

"What's this smell?" he asks.

"Oh, I had an accident at the gas station. Spilled gas all over myself."

"Isn't Animal Haven in the opposite direction?"

That's when the map app rats me out. "Please make a U-turn and proceed to the route."

"I suppose you're right."

"Why did you turn this way?"

"Er… mmm…" *To lose your tail* doesn't seem like a great answer. "I got confused."

"Is this vehicle yours, ma'am?"

"No, no. It's rented."

"I'll need to see your license and the rental agreement."

"Sure."

I take my driver's license out of my wallet and search in my bag for the rental contract. It's not there.

"Is there a problem?" the cop asks.

"I can't find the contract."

"Is that so?"

"I'm sure I had it in here somewhere."

"Ma'am, please step out of the car."

"What? No. I have it. It's here somewhere, I swear."

I drop the bag on the passenger seat and make a quick dash for the glove compartment. *Maybe I put it in there without realizing.*

That's when everything goes south. The officer jumps back and grabs the handle of the gun strapped to his belt.

"Stop!" he yells.

Hand still on the compartment handle, I freeze.

"Place both hands on the wheel," the policeman instructs me. "Slowly, and where I can see them."

What the hell? What does he think, that I have a gun hidden in my glove compartment? *Oh! That must be exactly what he's thinking.*

I comply and place both hands on the wheel. "You people are unbelievable. I was just searching for the rental agreement, and I don't have a gun. For your information, I'm against firearms."

"Ma'am, please step out of the car. And from now on, only *slow* movements."

"This is ridiculous. What are you going to do? *Arrest me?* I've done nothing wrong!"

The officer not-so-patiently sighs. "Ma'am, your car plate is registered to a blue Toyota Corolla, whereas you're driving a gray Hyundai Elantra. The plate recognition camera picked up the discrepancy as we drove behind you. And you're transporting an unrestrained animal apparently soaked in gasoline. Once again, please step out of the vehicle."

"I've told you the damn car is rented. It's not my fault if the rental company put the wrong plate on. And I've told you I just found the dog at a gas station and that I was bringing him to a shelter."

"But then we flash you and instead of pulling over you turn in the opposite direction. Don't make me ask again, please step out of the car."

The brute is only missing an "or else" at the end of the sentence. "Or what? What are you going to do?"

"Ma'am, step out of the car or you'll force me to call reinforcements." The officer taps the walkie-talkie strapped to his vest, close to his shoulder. "As of right now, you're resisting arrest."

"You're seriously arresting me? For what?" I open the door adding, "You're a big, uniformed bully." I get out of the car. "You can't do this. I'm an honest, tax-paying American citizen."

"Then you've nothing to fear."

"This is still a free country. You can't arrest me for no reason, it's an abuse of power."

"No, it's not. Please turn around, ma'am."

"Why?"

"Turn around."

I do as he says.

"Now place your hands on the back of your head."

"Are you handcuffing me? Is it really necessary?"

"Yes, ma'am. And I suggest you fully cooperate."

"Are you going to tell me I have the right to remain silent next?"

"You most definitely have that right, ma'am."

***

After a short journey spent handcuffed in the backseat of a police car with Mr. Mutt by my side, the cops bring me to a police station. Another officer asks me questions to fill out a personal information sheet and confiscates my watch and bag. A third policeman makes me sign a property log for my personal effects. No one takes my fingerprints or a mug shot, leaving me to wonder if I've really been arrested or if I'm only being held in custody.

Will I have a criminal record after today? For what? Renting a car? For saving a dog's life?

No one answers my questions. A female officer escorts me down a depressing cellblock and shows me into a cell. Mr. Mutt follows me around and nobody seems to mind so we're locked up together. Luckily, we're alone. No crazy cellmates.

I sit on a small cot bed—the only piece of furniture in this dump. Mr. Mutt lies next to me, resting his head on my thighs. Without my watch, it's hard to tell how much time is passing. How long will they keep us here? Will I get to make the famous phone call? Who should I call? I really don't wish for anyone to see me behind bars, especially not when I'm so dirty and smelly. I can't call my parents, they'd get a heart attack. *Nikki.* I'll call Nikki and ask her to find me a lawyer. It's my civil right to see a lawyer! The police can't keep me here indefinitely.

The rental company is so screwed. I'm so going to sue them. This mess is *their* fault! They mix up license plates and I end up in jail. *Jail,* more a tiny concrete hellhole with bars and no air. I'm getting cabin fever. I get up and pace around. Not that it helps. I can only take three steps wall-to-wall. How do people spend years caged like this? I've only been here a few hours and I'm already panicking. I need to know how long they'll keep me here.

Against my better judgment, I grab the bars and place my

face as close between two as I can without actually touching skin to metal. I peek down the hall to see if I can yell for someone to come explain my position.

That's when Richard appears on the hall threshold holding a folder.

"Well, well, well," the boss says, walking toward me.

It takes me a minute to believe he's not a hallucination. Of all the people I didn't want to see me at rock bottom, my impossibly sexy boss definitely tops the list.

"What are you doing here?" I ask.

"They finally tracked down the rental agreement, which was in the company's name." Richard stops in front of my cell. "So NYPD called the office to verify your story. Honestly, when the police called to say one of my employees had been arrested, I never imagined it'd be the office's Miss Goody Two-shoes."

Is that how Richard sees me? Like a prissy princess? To be fair, I spent years trying to cultivate exactly that image. Still, his words hurt.

"I'm a victim of the system," I complain.

"Let's see." Richard opens the folder. "Unruly conduct, resisting arrest, disorderly person's offense under animal cruelty laws," he reads the charges against me. "And driving with the wrong license plate!"

"The car is rented. And I was rescuing the dog from a guy who wanted to send him to pest control." Mr. Mutt barks his support. "Also, I haven't resisted arrest, as unjust and unnecessary as it was."

"It says in here you called the police officer trying to take you in 'a big, uniformed bully' and that you accused him of abuse of power."

"Can you please wipe that stupid"—*lips-magnet*—"grin from your face?"

"I'm sorry, but this is just too fun. Of all the dumb things you had on that list of yours, I never thought you'd tackle the getting-arrested one."

"You know about the list?" I ask in horror, releasing the bars and taking a step back.

Richard nods, still grinning.

I slap my forehead. "The night we met. So I didn't just talk about a list in general, I showed you the actual thing?"

"That you did."

"But you didn't tell anyone else about it, did you?"

"No, I promise. But me knowing is the least of your problems." He taps the folder. "I believe the city of New York now has it on record."

"Not funny."

"Not joking. It was in your bag." Richard searches the file with his eyes. "Item twenty-one, a crumpled sheet of paper."

I scowl at him. The sheer humiliation doesn't matter now. I'll worry about never being able to look the boss in the eye ever again later. First, let's get out of prison.

"Has everything been cleared with the plate?" I ask again.

"Yes, the rental company admitted it was their mistake."

"So they know I'm innocent! Why am I still in here?"

Richard can't help his lips from curling up as he speaks. "There's still the matter of the other misdemeanors."

"So what?" I collapse on the cot bed. "Are they keeping me here overnight?"

"The officer who took you in *kindly* agreed to let you off with a warning if… you apologize."

I shoot off the bed and grab the bars again. "Apologize? *Apologize?* They mistreat me. Arrest me for no good reason without reading me my rights. Then they keep me locked in here for hours without letting me speak to a lawyer or make a phone call… and *I* should apologize?"

"The officer had probable cause; a Miranda warning wasn't necessary. And since you haven't really been charged with anything yet, you didn't need a lawyer."

"Since when did you become such a legal expert? You're not even American."

"I came to the rescue with a lawyer friend. She's waiting for me outside."

She? I get a mental picture of a sleek, attractive femme fatale in stiletto heels. Like Kim Basinger in *LA Confidential.* Another *friend.*

"So what are my options?"

Richard shrugs. "If I were you, I'd suck it up, apologize, and go home to shower." He flares his nostrils for emphasis. "But if you want to spend the night in here with your furry inmate and face real charges, be my guest."

"Easy for you to say. You weren't mistreated."

"Now, you'd better decide," Richard says, turning his head toward the main entrance. "The officer in question is coming. Want me to wait and give you a lift home?"

Hell, no. The less time the boss spends with me while I'm this messed up the better. And I can't stand to meet his lawyer "friend" in this state either. "No, thank you. I'll call my roommate."

"See you tomorrow at the office, then."

Richard winks and walks away.

Mr. Mutt barks.

"I know," I say, patting the dog. "I like him, too."

***

By the time I get out of jail, it's already dark outside and the animal shelter is closed. The rental company has retrieved the car from the location of my arrest, and there's no cab or Uber in the world who'd take me for a ride while I'm this dirty. Not to mention the gasoline-soaked pup. Unfortunately, Nikki doesn't have a car—I only used that excuse to get rid of Richard. So I—we—have to walk home. Luckily, this morning I picked shoes comfortable enough to drive in so they're not too bad to walk in either, and my house is only a few blocks away.

On the way there, I stop at a Petsmart and buy all the dog-grooming products they carry. At home, I give Mr. Mutt a very long bath. Then I give the bath a thorough cleaning before finally showering myself, hoping to wash away not only the dirt, but today's humiliation as well. I'm dry and wearing PJs before Nikki comes home.

"Is that a dog on our couch?" my roommate asks as she comes into the apartment.

She's not wrong. I spent the last twenty minutes losing another battle of wills. It started with me saying Mr. Mutt wasn't allowed on the couch and ended with the puppy nestled in my lap.

"Yes."

"I thought you weren't an animal person. I've been begging you to get a cat for ages, you always said the house was too small for a pet, and now you bring home a dog?" Nikki sits on the coffee table, staring at us accusingly. "Does he have a name? Where did you find him?"

"I call him Mr. Mutt."

"That's a horrible name."

"And I found him at a Chevron…"

Mr. Mutt barks.

"…gas station. What's up with you?" I ask the dog.

Nikki studies him. "He barked when you said Chevron."

The pup barks again.

"Chevron?" I repeat.

And again.

"I think we settled that horrible Mr. Mutt name, right, Chevron?" Nikki asks.

"*Ar-rooff!*"

Nikki finally pats him. "So are we keeping him?"

"No."

An excruciating howl rips through the room.

"Oh, I forgot," I say. "The pup speaks English."

"Right," Nikki says skeptically. "So what is he doing here if he isn't staying?"

"The plan was to drop him at Animal Heaven, but by the time I got out of jail the shelter was closed. I couldn't leave him on the street."

Nikki is about to pet Chevron again when she stops, hand in midair. "Wait, reverse. *Jail?*"

"Yeah, jail…" I tell her of my afternoon of misery.

"Aw, so now Mr. Hot Sticker even saved you from prison."

"Richard didn't save me from prison. He just had to be there as a witness, and used it as an excuse to hook up with a lady lawyer."

Nikki scrunches her face. "Ouch."

"I don't care."

"Of course you don't. Just as much as we aren't keeping the puppy."

"*Woof!*"

Seven

Always Be Responsible

There's something bulgy on my bed that's preventing me from stretching my legs. *So annoying.* I ignore the nuisance for as long as I can until finally I blink my eyes open and find a set of big brown eyes fixated on me.

When Chevron notices I'm awake, he starts wagging his tail like mad. *Oh, right! I still need to take him to a shelter.* At five thirty in the morning, shelters must be closed, but it's not too early to take Chevron for a run.

"Let's see what you're made of," I tell him, getting up.

After putting on my running clothes and sneakers, I secure Chevron with the brand new leash I bought yesterday. The pup pants hah-hah-hah happily the entire time, his tail never sitting still. I reward him with a dog cookie and we exit the apartment.

As soon as we're outside, Chevron stops near a streetlight to relieve himself. Oh, crap! What if he has to go number two? I've nothing to pick it up with. Luckily, Chevron lowers his leg and looks up at me expectantly.

"Let's go."

"*Woof!*"

We make our way to the Hudson River. I start with a slow jog to see how Chevron copes as I'm not sure how malnourished he is. From the way he devoured his dinner yesterday, I'm guessing very.

Still, he seems able to keep up. I quicken my pace and he follows suit. Having this little ball of fur run at my feet makes me strangely blissful. Weird... running alone has always been my thing. Whenever a boyfriend or a friend asks to join me, I can't help but resent them. Feels like an intrusion on my special me-time. Running is a moment of self-reflection and liberation I usually want to spend alone. But today, having Chevron track alongside, I'm one-hundred percent glad for the company. And the puppy seems to enjoy the exertion just as much.

All the same, I cut the run short. I don't want to overwhelm this little guy.

Back home, I shower and search for shelters' hours as I eat breakfast. Most don't open until noon. I guess I could work from home in the morning and go to the office in the afternoon. Richard seems the kind of boss who'd be flexible about office hours. But I'd better make sure, so I text him to ask if it's okay, explaining the dog situation. My phone pings back at once with his reply.

> Why don't you bring the little guy with you?

As per my contacts renaming kink, Richard ended up as Jerry Maguire. The sexiest boss in chick flick history seemed like a good match for him.

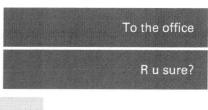

> To the office

> R u sure?

> Yeah

> A friend of mine runs a vet clinic here Brooklyn

I can take you both
there when it opens

Another *friend,* huh? Someone with long legs and batting lashes, I'm sure.

I type, "Okay, thanks," and end the text with a double paw emoji.

"Good news," I tell Chevron. "You're coming to the office with me."

"*Woof.*"

"All right, let's do this."

Before we leave, I check the subway website for regulations on dog transportation... And we're out of luck again. Apparently, all animals need to be inside a pet carrier to be allowed on trains.

"You know what? We're going to walk today. It's only two miles."

"*Ar rooff.*"

Nikki, clad in cat-print PJs, shuffles out of her room like a zombie and joins us at the kitchen bar.

"Is there coffee?" she asks.

I pour her a mug while an overexcited Chevron waggles his tail in welcome.

Nikki ignores him. "You're wasting your charms, little guy. I'm a cat person."

With a single cry, Chevron lays at her feet, subdued.

"She's joking," I console him.

"I'm not," Nikki insists.

Chevron wails again and nuzzles her bare feet with his wet nose.

Nikki tries to remain aloof, but her resolve breaks. "All right." She leans down to pat Chevron's head, and the good pup tries to jump into her lap. Nikki pets him a little longer and then asks, "So what's the deal with the dog?"

When I tell her of my plans with Richard, she raises an eyebrow at me. I wish I knew how to do that skeptical expression. If I tried to raise just one brow in a sassy way, I'd end up looking ridiculous.

"No comment," Nikki says.

"Why? What's wrong?"

"Nothing, just saving the 'I told you so' for later."

"What exactly did you tell me?"

"That the dog is staying... Hmm, what else?" Nikki gives me a shrewd look to clue me into the fact that she's really talking about Richard. I play dumb, so she adds, "Anyway, I'll be gone tonight."

"Where to this time?" Video marketing is the best job; she gets to travel so much.

"Just upstate for the night; gotta get ready. The crew is picking me up in"—she looks at her watch—"twenty minutes."

Nikki turns around the bar and hugs me goodbye then bends down to scratch Chevron behind the ears. The puppy is so ecstatic that he follows her to her room.

I go after them and turn right instead of left to reach my bedroom. Since I have to walk, I change into a pair of pants and a blouse so that I can wear gym shoes for the crossing to Brooklyn without appearing too weird. Foldable flats do the trick only for short trips. I grab my duffel bag from under the bed where it's been since my breakup with Gerard, and put together a basic dog-at-the-office survival kit. A bag of dog cookies, a bowl for food, another bowl for water, and, for me, a pair of high-wedged pink All Stars. No matter if I'm in sportswear, no one can see me without heels. At the last minute, I add a bundle of plastic bags.

There. Now I'm ready for any doggy situation.

***

As soon as Chevron steps a paw into the office, he becomes the center of attention. I leave him with grungy Saffron and vintage Ada to go drop the duffel bag at my workstation.

There's a big bowl of oranges placed on the desk. *How odd.* I'm about to take out Chevron's water bowl and fill it when Hugo, the ginger News Editor, comes near my desk with two weird metallic mugs.

"Want some coffee?" he asks, offering me one.

"Oh, wow. Thanks." Hugo never makes me coffee. Where does the extra-nice attitude come from?

As I bring the mug to my lips, it feels like everyone is watching me. Like one of those slow motion moments in sitcoms where all the actors are holding their breath, waiting for something to happen. My eyes finally focus on the black writing on the side of the mug: USP ALCATRAZ. I lower the cup, aghast, and everyone starts laughing. They *were* watching me. That's also when Indira spins in her chair, showing the front of her bright orange T-shirt. It spells, "I want to be your prison wife."

My entire body heats. Not just my face, but my neck and shoulders all flare bright red. Everything makes sense now. The oranges, the mug, the suspense… they know I've been in jail. Damn Richard, I'm going to strangle him!

"Very funny," I say. And the laughter doubles.

I have to endure half an hour of prison jokes before Richard appears. "How are our two inmates doing today?" he greets Chevron and me.

I scowl at him.

"Still ruffled, are we?"

"I'd like to see how happy you'd be after being unjustly arrested and made to apologize for it," I reply pettily.

"You should write an article about police brutality," Indira suggests, unable to hide the amusement in her voice.

"Nice shirt," Richard tells her.

She winks. "Thanks, boss."

I roll my eyes and hide under my desk to pat Chevron, who promptly nudges my calves in support.

"So." Richard squats down next to us, eyes level with mine.

For a moment, all the air leaves my lungs. Finding myself almost nose-to-nose with Richard is giving me heart palpitations. When will he stop having this effect on me?

"Want to check out the clinic?" the boss asks, scratching Chevron behind the ears.

The treacherous dog forgets all about me and goes to nuzzle Richard's face. And for the first time in my life, I'm jealous of a quadruped.

***

The veterinary clinic is only a ten-minute walk from the office, but as our trio strolls down the streets of Brooklyn, I can't help noticing the seething looks of envy New Yorker women send my way. Walking with Richard and a happy puppy, I must look like I'm living the dream. If only the ladies knew how far from picture-perfect my life really is.

Needless to say, the vet is female. Not only that, she greets us with a perfect smile worthy of a toothpaste commercial. Actually, her general wholesomeness would play well in a family friendly advert. With big blue eyes, chestnut hair, and rosy cheeks, she's an image of friendly beauty—particularly friendly toward Richard.

As she comes out from behind the admission desk, her

cheeks become rosier, her smile broadens—*how is that even possible? How many teeth does she have?*—and her eyes sparkle with something that could only be described as utter adoration. So the vet, too, has a crush on the boss. Have they dated in the past? Is everything Indira said true? Has Richard literally left a trail of broken hearts sprinkled all over New York?

After greeting us and introducing herself as Michelle, the vet shifts her entire attention to Chevron. Not even Richard's Bambi-like eyes can compete with real puppy eyes.

Michelle picks Chevron up and cuddles him. "And who do we have here?" The puppy loves the attention and yaps and nuzzles in response. "Good boy, oh, you're such a good boy."

As Michelle walks away with my dog, an explicable pang of something makes my throat tighten. Okay, no need to get territorial. Not over Richard and not over the dog—*who's not your dog, by the way, as there's no way you can keep him.* Begrudgingly, I follow the vet into an examination room.

With Chevron placed on a metal table, Michelle asks me an infinite series of questions—most of which I have no clue how to answer—and then she tells us she needs to do a full checkup. The clinic closes at six in the evening and Chevron will be ready for pickup after four.

Even if I know I'm going to see him in just a few hours, I get withdrawal syndrome symptoms as early as my first step away from the room. His desperate cries following us as we leave don't help either.

Richard must notice because he tries to distract me with conversation. "You actually named the dog after the gas station?" he asks as we walk back to the office.

"Every time someone said Chevron he barked, what was I supposed to do?"

"That fur ball is so adorable, he makes me want to go to a shelter and adopt a little guy just like him."

"No need for a shelter, you can adopt exactly *him*."

Richard stops dead in the street and turns toward me. "You're not keeping him?"

"Even if I wanted to, there's no way I can."

"Why not?"

"My apartment is too small, I'm out all day, and I don't have a car."

"You could bring him to the office. He could become our mascot. And since when is a car essential to having a dog?"

"For one, he's not allowed on the subway."

"How did you come to work today?"

"We walked."

"All the way from Manhattan?" Richard seems impressed, and we start walking again. "You could've told me. I would've picked you up."

I wave him off. "It's no big deal."

"So what are you going to do with the puppy?"

"I'm bringing him to a shelter... unless you want him."

"He's not going to a bloody shelter."

This time I stop. "What else am I supposed to do? I'm only being responsible here."

"That's your problem. Maybe you should put more heart into what you do!"

I gasp. "That's rich coming from you."

"Me, why?"

"Because you should take your own advice."

"Meaning?"

"Put your heart in what you do."

"And where did you get the notion that my heart is not in what I do?"

"Maybe from the fact that in the short time I've worked for you, you've dated—what? Three, four different women? And the vet seems like another old flame."

Richard doesn't deny it. A dark shadow crosses his face, and he flashes me a hard, reproachful glare. "How I spend my time outside the office is none of your business. You've no place passing judgment on my personal life."

"Neither is it any of your business if I want to adopt a dog or not, and you shouldn't judge me if I say I can't. Again, take your own advice." With that, I march away, quickening my pace without waiting for my stupid boss.

***

Even if we don't say another word to each other for the rest of the day, the moment I get up to leave the office, Richard joins me.

He stops next to me as I wait for the elevator. "I'm coming with you," he threatens, and I don't dare retort.

Wrapped in a heavy silence, we walk back toward the clinic.

Until Richard breaks. "I should apologize for earlier; it wasn't my place to talk to you the way I did."

"I'm sorry, too. Same as you said."

"So we're good?" Richard asks, staring dead ahead.

"Yeah, we're good."

Tension lingers. We were both out of line earlier. Still, I appreciate Richard apologizing first.

At the clinic, I bear witness once again to Michelle's love-struck attitude toward the boss. And it's a good ten minutes before she notices I'm even there and brings us to see Chevron.

"So how's he doing?"

"Our puppy is actually a she," Michelle informs us.

"You're a girl?" I ask Chevron, who's back on the table

68

chasing her tail in circles and yapping. I focus on Michelle. "Anything else?"

"She's slightly underweight for her age and she was malnourished and a bit dehydrated. Anyway, we gave her fluids, and a good diet with plenty of love should cure the rest."

I bite my lower lip. "Right."

"You don't seem convinced?"

Tears already prickle my eyes. "It's just that I don't think I can keep her."

Chevron stops running and lays flat on the table, resting her head on her front paws while whining.

I explain my situation to Michelle and in response, she informs me of all the programs New York City offers to pet owners in need. Reduced routine veterinary care, reduced pet boarding fee, free supplies, and she even gives me a few names of trusted dog-sitting services.

"But ultimately it's your decision," Michelle concedes.

"What if I helped you?" Richard blurts out.

An unwise ecstasy grips me as I listen to Richard trying to convince me to keep Chevron, advertising all the things he could do to help. The more my mood brightens, the more Michelle's face darkens. She seems annoyed with us. The Most-friendly-girl-on-Earth starts getting snippy, and unceremoniously ushers us out of the clinic claiming she has to close. Even if it's still twenty to six.

Just outside, there's a small park. Seems like a good place to reflect on what to do. We sit down on a bench. Chevron jumps up and sits quietly, resting her snout on my thigh. Her big, scared eyes stare into mine.

Richard looks at her and asks, "How can you think of abandoning her?"

I shake my head, close to tears. "I can't. But how can I keep her? I could walk to work every day now that the weather is warm. But what about winter? I can't walk two miles in the freezing rain or snow across a bridge. She'd get too wet and cold; it wouldn't be good for her."

"I could drive you home when the weather is too bad to walk."

I stare into Richard's brown eyes, not daring to let my hopes rise too high. "You'd pick me up and drive me home every time it rains or snows? This is New York, Richard. Awful weather is pretty much a given in winter. And traffic is just awful."

"For a cutie like this one"—he pokes Chevron's nose—"in a heartbeat."

As though conscious of her fate being discussed, Chevron nuzzles my hand with her moist muzzle and whines. How did I get so attached to her in less than a day? Yesterday, I didn't know she existed, and now, the thought of living without her is too heartbreaking to even consider. But I have to think of Chevron's best interest. Be responsible.

"So why don't you keep her full time?" I ask.

"I'm often away for the weekend, and I go back to England at least twice a year. I wouldn't be able to manage a dog full time."

"Mmm…"

"Come on, the solution is right here. I can cover for you when you're away and drive you home if the weather is awful… or you could borrow my car. Or she could stay at my place sometimes. Or, even better, you could move to Brooklyn."

Over my dead body. Sorry Chevron, but I can't leave Manhattan, not even for you. *Yeah, right!*"

"Why not?"

"I don't know, Richard. What if I change jobs? What would happen then?"

The boss smiles a bitter smile. "Already sending out CVs?"

"That's not what I meant. A dog is a ten-year commitment at the very minimum. And it's not as if we can decide to keep her now and change our minds in five, ten, or maybe even fifteen years. What if you move back to England? What if one or both of us moves away from New York?"

"We'll figure something out. You really want to bring Chevron to a shelter?"

I shake my head. "No, but the responsible thing would be to find her a forever family that will adopt her."

"Then don't be responsible. Live a little. What if no one adopts her? You want her to stay caged up forever?"

The same cabin fever from the few hours I spent in jail makes my pulse race. I can't send Chevron to live in a cage. Not even for a day.

"No!"

"So let's keep her. If we join forces, we can."

"Are you really ready for this kind of responsibility?"

"I am, if you are."

I stare into two pairs of puppy-dog eyes and there's no way I can say no. "Okay then." I could be going crazy, but Richard's enthusiasm is infectious.

Richard smiles, too. "So you want to leave her with me tonight?"

"No!" Instinctively, I put a hand on Chevron's head as if to protect her. "I mean, it's only May. The weather's great. She can stay with me for now."

"So you're going to walk to work every day?"

"Or bike. I'll do it instead of running."

Richard smiles again and shakes his head.

"What?"

"You're never letting go of that dog, you know that, right?"

I start to protest, but he cuts me short. "Come on," he says, jumping up from the bench and offering me his hands. "Let's go."

As I walk home over the Manhattan Bridge, I can't help the little smile pulling at my lips. I know Richard offered to help only for Chevron's sake, but still, he was ready to commit to us—okay, to her—for an undisclosed number of years. All Indira's theories about his phobia must be exaggerated. All the boss needs is a little push…

Eight

Always Dress Properly

The need to walk to work forces me to tone down my wardrobe and sort of embrace the athleisure movement. So today my outfit—a pale pink scuba-jersey sweatshirt, shiny paneled leggings, and the irreplaceable pink wedge All Stars—gains me a wink of approval from Indira as soon as I round my desk.

"Cool outfit, girl," she greets me. "The boss wants to see you."

After setting down Chevron's food and water bowls, I knock on Richard's door.

"Come in," he says, voice muffled by the glass.

I poke my head in. "You wanted to see me?"

"Ah, Blair, yes." Richard beckons me, and I sit in the chair opposite to his desk.

Today he's wearing a deep blue shirt that's begging to be ripped off him. I swallow.

"This is a bit last minute, but are you free this weekend?" Richard asks.

My heart skips a beat.

Is he asking me on a date? What do I say?

"This weekend?" I repeat trying to buy time to think.

"Yep. How would you feel about flying with me to LA?"

A weekend in California? *That sounds so romantic.* Is this really happening?

"We would have to fly economy as the company budget is low…"

Company budget? *Oh.* My heart plummets. So it's a work thing. Stupid me for thinking otherwise.

"Sorry, I'm not following," I say. "Why LA?"

"A good friend of mine is hosting a charity ball in Los Angeles… You know Christian Slade?"

"Christian Slade?" My eyes bulge out. "As in the mega Hollywood star?"

"Yes, him."

"He's your friend?"

"Yes, we go way back. We met at boarding school in England."

"Wow!" Richard really is connected, Indira was right. "Why do you want me to come?"

"The event will be A-list celebrities only, with a red carpet and everything. I thought as Fashion Editor you could piece together a few nice articles…"

"Something like best and worst dressed…"

"To be honest, I'd like to give Christian's charity better exposure through a more commercial approach."

"Make the ladies lust over the Hollywood glam to spread the word about the cause?"

"Exactly."

I lean forward in my chair and switch from deluded-employee-helplessly-in-love-with-her-too-handsome-boss to professional magazine editor. "What's the name of the charity?"

"Teachers without Postcodes."

Opening my notepad, I scribble the name down to research later. "Interesting name. What's the cause?"

"A program to bring better school systems to kids in neighborhoods with underfunded education. The charity supports a network of charter schools."

"That's a great mission. Do you have a list of the attendees?"

"Yeah, I'll email it to you."

"What about interviews? Am I allowed to ask the guests questions, like when they reach the end of the red carpet, or something?"

"Let me double check with Chris, but I'm sure it won't be an issue."

I put a checkmark next to interviews. "And for photos?"

"How good is your phone's camera?"

I stare up from the pad. "Seriously?"

"You can buy freelance shots with the budget you have, no extras. The plane ticket and hotel will already be expensive enough."

"I can't do a spread without professional photos."

"Isn't Saskia's page still bringing in loads of ad revenue?"

"Yeah, but I've allocated the profits to other projects. What am I supposed to do?"

"Be creative. I don't like to micromanage my staff."

I suppress a scream of frustration.

"What about the fundraising?" I ask. Attending a black tie event like this can't be cheap. "Who pays for that?"

"The fee comes out of my pockets. I believe in the cause and I'm happy to support it."

Oh, so Richard has a Good-Samaritan side, too. *Not fair.* "That's very generous of you. When do we leave?"

"Friday, mid-afternoon. With the time change, we should get to California in time for dinner."

Dinner? You and me alone? *My palms get sweaty.*

"Is Chevron going to be okay?" Richard asks. "Can you leave her with someone? Or I could ask Michelle if she can board her."

"No, no. It's fine. My roommate will take care of her."

"Great. You can go home Friday at lunch, get Chevron settled, and meet me at the airport."

"Sure."

"Please ask Indira to sort the tickets and hotel. The gala is Saturday night; we can fly back Sunday on whatever flight costs less."

"Perfect. I'll sort everything with Indira." I get up to exit his office.

"Ah, Blair…"

"Mmm?"

"Not that I need to say it, but the dress code is formal. Bring a gown."

"And here I was thinking of borrowing one of Saffron's T-shirts."

Richard smiles and waves me out of his office.

I sit at my desk, unable to wipe a little satisfied smile from my lips. An entire weekend alone with Richard. A two-night stay in the same hotel, dinner, and a gala. *It means nothing.* No, but still. We could walk along the Santa Monica pier at sunset, and we're going to a Hollywood ball together. Anything could happen…

"What are you daydreaming about?" Indira says from beside me.

"Nothing." Despite myself, I blush. *Busted.*

"So what did the boss want?"

"Oh, right. There's a charity event this Saturday in LA, with celebrities and everything. Richard wants me to do a fashion-slash-gossip report and asked if you could book our tickets and hotel."

Indira scrutinizes me for a long moment. "What did I tell you on your first day here?"

I stare at my sweatshirt and grab the hem. "I thought you liked this outfit, isn't it casual enough?"

"Wrong one. You've nailed the 'dress more casually.' It's the 'don't fall for the boss' you're having issues with."

"I-I haven't… you don't know what you're t-talking about," I stutter.

"Yeah, right. Should I book adjoining rooms?" She flashes me an evil grin.

I crumple up a sheet of paper and throw it at her. "You're wicked."

The ball rolls off Indira's desk, and Chevron promptly chases after it.

Indira shakes her head. "And you're in so much trouble, girl."

***

When I get home that night, Nikki is already back from her trip upstate.

"Oh, see... the dog is still living here," Nikki says and makes jazz hands. "Surprise."

When Chevron hears her voice, she yaps and jumps onto the couch, nuzzling Nikki's face. Good girl, buttering Nikki up. She doesn't know about my agreement with Richard to share custody, and she'll have plenty to say about our new canine roommate. But right now, she's too busy making cute voices at Chevron.

"Good boy," Nikki coos. "You're such a good boy."

"Actually," I say, sitting on the coffee table in front of them. "Chevron's a girl."

"A girl? We need a pink leash, then."

"Yeah, when she gets a little bigger, I'll get her a new one."

"When she gets bigger, huh?" Nikki gives me a smug *told you so* smirk. "So we're keeping her?"

"Well..." I explain my custody agreement with Richard and her face becomes more smug by the second. "Can you please wipe that self-satisfied expression from your face?"

"No, honey. Honestly, I didn't think you had it in you."

"Had what in me?"

"The cold blood to use this cutie"—she ruffles Chevron's ears, making them fly up and down—"to reel in a man."

"I'm not using Chevron to wheel anyone anywhere. Richard just offered to help me take care of her so she wouldn't have to go to a shelter or be put up for adoption."

"Oh, so you haven't fantasized about romantic walks down Central Park hand-in-hand with the boss?"

"No, I haven't," I lie through my teeth.

Nikki flashes me a skeptical smirk but doesn't call me out. "Besides adopting a dog together, how's it going with Mr. Hot?"

"He's bringing me to LA for the weekend."

"No! I mean, how?"

"Promise you won't freak out…"

She does the Girl Scout salute.

"Richard's taking me to a charity gala and wants me to cover the red carpet."

"And why should I freak out?"

"It's Christian Slade's charity ball."

Nikki sags against the couch backrest. "You lucky biatch!"

"I know."

"Can I hide in your luggage, please?"

"Eh, here's the thing…" I'm glad she hasn't stopped cuddling Chevron for one second since we came home. "Would you take care of our new roomie this weekend?"

"Oh, so you get to go to California with your hot boss to a party hosted by the sexiest man alive and I'm stuck here with this fur ball?"

"*Woof,*" Chevron yaps, and licks her cheek.

It works, Nikki's already a goner.

"I'll do it."

"You're the be—"

The buzzer interrupts me.

"I didn't order take out," Nikki says.

"No, it's for me."

"Who is it?"

"Mandy, from Angelika Black. They're lending me the dress for the gala."

"How come a major designer is giving you a dress?"

"They love me after I picked them for the Saskia Landon shoot."

"Life's unfair."

I buzz Mandy in and help her carry the wheeled garment rack from the elevator into our apartment, along with the six black garment bags it's carrying. Fashion lust makes my fingers prickle. I can't wait to pull down the zippers and discover the designer treasures inside.

As we drag the rack into the living room, Chevron jumps off the couch and barks to welcome the newcomer.

Mandy's reaction to our puppy isn't exactly warm. "These gowns are extremely delicate." She wrinkles her nose. "I'm not sure having a dog around as you try them on is a good idea."

Chevron stops yapping and goes to sit quietly on the rug in the faraway corner of the living room. She's the image of a well-behaved puppy.

Mandy raises her brows.

"Chevron understands English," I explain.

"Well." Mandy's face illuminates in a big smile. "The dog can watch from over there. So"—she turns toward me—"want to have a look at what I brought?"

I attack the zippers and reveal six stunning gowns. Yet the one furthest to the right catches my eye at once. It's a flowy dress in the exact pale jade shade of my eyes. The textile plays with tulle and lace in an illusion of transparencies and is covered in lace flower appliqués. The V of the neck plunges deep, making the gown slightly scandalous. And the long skirt flows to the floor, ethereal and lovely.

Registering my expression, Mandy says, "And who said love at first sight isn't a thing? Want to try it on?"

I nod.

She carefully takes it off the hanger and hands it over.

The fabric is soft in my hands, like the consistency of a cloud. I walk into my room feeling as if I, too, were as light as air. At the speed of light, I peel off my clothes and then carefully pull the gown on, cautious not to pinch the delicate tulle anywhere. After some contortions, I manage to pull up the zipper on my own. I complete the look with a pair of heels and stare transfixed at the results in the mirror. A-mazing. A dream translated into fabric. But on my short frame, the neckline drops so deep it reaches almost below my ribcage. I swallow. It's indecent.

As perfect as the dress is, it can't be worn in public. At least not by me. I'm tempted to strip it off right away, but pulling down the zipper proves more complicated than pulling it up. And I don't want to risk tearing the tulle anywhere. I've no idea what this gown costs, but I'm sure I can't afford it.

Shyly, I step back into the living room.

Nikki gasps. "You look amazing."

Mandy's assessment is more professional. "Fits you like a glove. We only need to shorten the skirt by three or four inches."

"Well, yeah. Except for the fact that all this dress says about me is, 'hello, meet my breasts.'"

"Seriously, sweetheart?" Mandy arches an eyebrow. "You're going to Hollywood. You'll still look like a nun."

"I doubt this is nun-wear, even in LA. This is the kind of dress you have to double tape to keep everything in place."

"So it's a bit more revealing than what you're used to," Nikki says. "What's the big deal?"

"I can't show up at work like this."

"Come on," Nikki insists. "It's not work."

"But Richard will be there!"

"The more reason to wear the dress."

Mandy injects herself into the conversation. "Is there a

gentleman involved?"

"No," I reply, just as Nikki says, "Yes."

"Then you must definitely choose this one," Mandy concludes, taking Nikki's word over mine.

"Definitely," my nasty roommates agrees.

"Or maybe I should try on one of the other dresses..." I take a more conservative-looking black gown off the rack. "This looks much more—"

"Safe," Nikki ends the phrase for me.

"I was going to say appropriate. Come on, Nikki," I protest one last time. "This is not me."

"That's exactly my point."

"What do you mean?"

"This dress was totally made for the new you. If you can go to jail, you can wear the dress."

Mandy is looking at us as if we're crazy. "You went to jail?"

I jump to reassure her. "It was a bureaucratic misunderstanding. I wasn't really arrested."

Her expression relaxes.

Nikki pushes her point, "There must be something on your not-to-do list of things you have to do that forces you to wear this beauty."

I mentally scroll through the items and smile devilishly. "Always dress appropriately...?"

"Then it's decided!" Nikki's smile is almost as wicked as mine.

Mandy nods her approval, but it's Chevron's bark of endorsement that seals the deal.

Nine

Never Confide in Strangers

I shouldn't be so early. Simple as that. There are a million reasons to keep a decent buffer when traveling, but I should've kept it practical. Three hours for a domestic flight is an eternity. Even the monstrous departures board of JFK informs me I'm definitely too early. No gate info yet.

I need to find somewhere cozy to wait. The only place with seats in sight of the board is an airport bar, so I drag my suitcase along and sit on a stool at the counter.

"Hi," the bartender—a friendly looking blonde-hair-blue-eye type with a warm expression—greets me. "What can I get you?"

"Something to drink, please," I say.

"Cocktail, beer, a soda?"

"No thanks. Do you have any organic juices or a relaxing tea?"

The bartender's blue eyes twinkle. "Let's see." He squats behind the counter to open a fridge, I assume. "On the organic shelf, there's OJ, Honeycrisp apple juice, carrot beet ginger juice, or mango tea."

"The carrot ginger, please."

Mr. Friendly & Cute shakes the bottle and pours the juice into a tall glass. "Here you go."

"Thanks." I take a sip and check my watch.

"Waiting for someone?" the bartender asks.

"Yeah."

"Are they late?"

"No, I'm early."

"Better safe than sorry. When does your plane leave?"

"In three hours."

He raises an eyebrow. "International?"

I shake my head.

The bartender lets out a low whistle. "That's a big buffer for a national flight," he says, and then pours me some tortilla chips.

The poor guy hasn't asked why I'm so early, and Mr. Cute here probably doesn't care, but I don't know why I start spilling out all the details of my personal life. "Truth is, I have to go on a business trip with my boss. We're going to LA for the weekend and I was nervous about this whole away-with-the-boss thing. So I came to the airport super early. Just in case. One never knows when traffic will go crazy in this city."

"Is your boss the fastidious type?"

"No, no. Nothing like that. I'm probably more fastidious than him."

The bartender chuckles. "So what is it?"

Totally against my will, my cheeks heat up, and I try to hide the blushing by taking another sip of juice.

"Ah." The bartender smiles knowingly. "I see. You have a crush on your boss?"

No point in denying it. Mr. Cute knows.

"Can I at least ask your name before I tell you all my darkest secrets?"

"Mark Cooper, pleased to meet you."

Mark offers me a hand and I shake it. "Blair Walker. Nice to meet you, too."

"So, this boss…" Mark lets the phrase hang.

"Do you ask all your patrons about their private lives?"

"Occupational hazard, I guess."

Again, his kind expression compels me to talk. "Yes, I sort of have a crush on my boss."

"Mmm…"

"And we're going to LA for the weekend," I continue.

"For?"

"A charity gala."

"Oh, black tie event?"

"Mm-hmm."

"What do you do for a living?"

"I run the women's section of an online magazine." I hand him a business card. Never miss an opportunity to market. "You should check us out."

Mark takes it. "Inceptor Magazine. Cool name."

"Yeah, Richard picked it."

"Richard the forbidden boss?"

"The one and only."

"So tell me." Mark leans his elbows on the counter. "What are the obstacles for this impossible love story? Is the boss-man already taken?"

We chat a little and I explain the situation, even including the sordid details of the first time I talked to Richard—at least the one time I remember.

"So you're hoping something will happen this weekend?" Mark asks when I'm finished.

I shrug. I don't know what I do or should hope. From the moment the boss asked me on this trip, I've spent countless hours daydreaming about what *could* happen. Dinner *à deux* by the ocean, dancing at the ball—very *Beauty and the Beast* in my head—bookended by Richard whisking me off my feet at the end of the night. In reality, I'm pretty sure nothing is going to happen. This is just business for him. I wouldn't be surprised if he brought a Californian date along for the evening. *Oh, the horror… what if he does?*

"Are you still here?" Mark interrupts my mental rant.

"Yeah, sorry." I'm about to explain my inner turmoil when my phone beeps, startling me. "It's Richard, he's here."

"Please tell him to join you," Mark begs. "I have to meet this guy."

"You can't say anything," I warn.

He does a zipper-over-the-mouth gesture. "My lips are sealed."

"Do you mind if I change shoes?"

Mark seems surprised by the question. "Please, go ahead."

I climb down from the stool and swap flats for spiky black pumps.

"Whoa." Mark's eyes widen when my head comes back level with his. "You shot up... like... five inches!"

"That's the whole point." I store my ballerinas inside the hand luggage, close the zipper, and sit back on the stool.

I wring my hands together until Mark places a warm, dry hand on top of mine and says, "Relax. You don't want to spook the boss." He smiles encouragingly.

When he lets go, I force my hands apart and dry my sweaty palms on my skirt. "Do I look okay?"

"You look perfect. The guy's a fool if he doesn't notice."

"Blair." Richard's voice makes me jolt. "There you are. I thought I was early, but you beat me."

"Hi, Richard." Even if I see him every day, my pulse starts racing and I suspect my cheeks are once again matching my red hair.

Mark winks and buys me some time to recover. "Hello there, can I get you something to drink?"

Richard scratches his head. "What are you having?" he asks me.

"Organic carrot beet ginger juice."

"Erm, sounds delicious." The boss tries not to make a too-disgusted face and turns toward Mark. "A pint of lager please."

Mark's lips twitch. "I only have American-sized pints if that's okay?"

"You shoddy Americans." Richard laughs and Mark chuckles along. At once, it's like they're old friends who've been running the I-am-American-you-are-British joke between them for years. This Mark guy really has a way with people.

Right at this moment, my mind's whizzing with unspeakable thoughts so I let Mark entertain Richard while I enjoy the view. The boss didn't shave before coming here. His jaw is already sporting a five o'clock shadow, making him even sexier than usual. From the way he casually places his sunglasses on top of his head, to the way he now rolls up the sleeves of his shirt—making me stare like the little pervert I am—everything about Richard exudes sex appeal. The only flaw being that lingering sadness behind his eyes. The one he works so hard to hide.

When he's halfway through his beer, Richard's phone rings. He looks at the screen and smiles apologetically. "I've got to take this," he says, walking away.

"Well." Mark smirks scratching his short beard. "I'm not an expert on guys, but the dude has charm. So what's your plan for the weekend?"

I shrug. "Survive without embarrassing myself too much?"

"That sounds like an awful plan."

"You have a better suggestion?"

"Live and embarrass yourself the most you can."

"Meaning?"

"Tell him how you feel."

A speaker in the background announces our flight.

"No way!" My stomach drops at the mere idea. "Shh, he's coming back."

"They announced our flight," Richard says, and chugs the

remaining half of his beer. "How much for everything?" he asks Mark.

Mark gives him the bill, and Richard pays for my juice as well. We both say goodbye to Mark, and I catch a furtive wink from my new bartender bestie as I stroll after Richard.

The boss frowns at me. "Collecting admirers?" he asks, as we walk toward our gate.

"What?"

"That bloke was all over you."

"Who?"

"Blue eyes, standing behind the bar."

"I seriously doubt that."

"He winked at you."

Oh, so the boss caught that. *Panic! He knows.* But then I remind myself that there's no way Richard could know Mark and I were talking about him. Let him assume Mark's wink was about how much the bartender liked me and not how much I like my boss.

I shrug and stop in front of our gate. "Mark is a friendly guy."

"Mark? Is that why you were holding hands when I arrived?"

Richard stops next to me and gives me a once-over, his eyes lingering long enough to give me goose bumps.

"We… I mean, what?"

Is the boss annoyed because he thinks I'm behaving unprofessionally? No, Richard isn't prissy like that.

So what then? Could he be acting… *jealous?* No. No way. *Blair, repeat after me: "You are on a business trip."* But I'm not the one getting all worked up over a stupid wink. And he's ogling my shoes.

Richard's eyes travel back up my body, stopping when they meet mine. "Do you always fly dressed like this?"

Okay, I admit I made a bit of an effort. In my defense, it

wasn't to seduce the boss. After only a few days, I was so fed up with the athleisure style, I couldn't wait to put on an elegant dress. And this little black midi dress is nothing too provocative. Maybe it's the shoes. The super narrow, super high stiletto heels must be eye-catching. Richard was openly staring at my feet just a moment ago.

"Well, since I didn't have to walk for once," I finally reply.

Richard's gaze flickers to the ground again, and I suppress a tiny smile. Are shoes his weak spot?

Ten

Never Make Exceptions

By the time we land, I'm so over the shoes. As gorgeous as my pumps are, I can't wait to kick them off. No matter that I've been sitting the entire time; these shoes were not made for pressure-bloated feet. Outside LAX, we hop in a cab to reach our hotel, and I have to muster all my willpower not to kick the stilettos off during the ride and reach for the flats in my suitcase. No pain, no height.

Indira chose a nice hotel in Santa Monica, near the ocean and with a stunning view of the pier. We check in and agree to meet in the lobby in an hour for dinner. The room is cozy if a little nondescript—a typical hotel chain with standardized furniture. But the view is everything.

A quick shower, and it's already time to get ready for the night. To pack light, I've picked out all my outfits in advance. The designated one for tonight is a sheath bandage dress in a shimmering metallic gold-bronze. The bandage's horizontal stripes and thick fabric are body-sculpting and make sure everything hangs just right.

But the real stars of this outfit are the shoes. As I take them out of their travel bag, I smirk. If Richard liked my pumps, wait until he sees these beauties. Knee-high metallic sandals with eight narrow straps, toes-to-knee, of which I have to individually buckle the last six. Not a quick job, but worth the trouble.

The soles are cushioned enough for me not to need gel inserts. Since the shoes are already such a statement, I keep the makeup light and natural.

In the lobby, I'm rewarded for my efforts with a long stare at my lower legs and two raised brows as I walk down the hall to meet Richard.

I smile. "Hey."

"Hey, yourself," Richard says. "Fancy dinner near the beach?"

"Couldn't think of a better place."

If May in New York is mild, in California it's already summer. I don't have much time to enjoy the warm evening breeze, however, as we hop in a cab right outside the hotel.

Richard gives the driver the name of a restaurant and we zip off into traffic.

"You know why Indira picked a hotel in Santa Monica when the gala is downtown?" he asks.

I suspect it was her idea of a joke. The beach being more romantic than skyscrapers.

I pretend to be clueless. "She said no one comes to LA to sleep downtown."

Richard doesn't ask me any other questions, and I'm too on edge to spark a conversation. The protracted silence makes the journey seem even longer. By the time the driver pulls over, we could've traveled from New York to Philadelphia for all I know. But I guess LA has a different spread than Manhattan. Everything seems broader here.

The driver kills the engine. "Sorry, but you'll have to walk from here. The boardwalk is pedestrians-only."

I step out of the cab, breathing in the sea air. Our destination looks a lot like the pan shots they do of Venice Beach in movies, even if I'm sure we're in Some-Other-Name Beach. Wooden buildings litter the concrete promenade on one side. On the other, it's tall palms, then sand, and finally the ocean where the last sunlight is sinking below the horizon.

Richard leads the way to… *oh, no. No!* A steakhouse. Story of my life. Guys love meat, and I'm a vegetarian. Maybe we'll skip the whole why-don't-you-eat-meat-oh-I-could-never-live-without-bacon drill. I'll order the one pasta dish on the menu, politely decline Richard's suggestion of bone-in filet or New York strip, saying I'm not in the mood for a steak, and I might get away with it.

That chance shatters five minutes after we're seated when a server arrives at our table parading a tray of bloody cuts and starts explaining the various merits of the differently sliced cadavers.

The sight of raw meat makes me slightly nauseous, so I sip some water to stop my stomach from heaving.

Richard notices. "Are you okay?"

"Mm-hmm," I mutter, staring away from the tray of death. "Could we skip the visual presentation, though?"

The server gives me the I-know-what-you-are-you'll-order-the-cheap-pasta-and-cut-my-tip-in-half evil eye, but he takes the hint and shuffles away.

Richard blinks. "What's the matter?"

"I sort of… don't eat meat."

"Like ever?"

No point in circling around it. "I'm vegetarian."

Richard scoffs. "You should've said something. We could've switched places. I thought vegetarians were supposed to tell you."

Now I get touchy. "Why? Did you introduce yourself saying, 'Hi, I'm Richard. I'm carnivorous'?"

"I was talking about the joke."

"What joke?"

"How do you know if someone is a vegetarian?"

I stare at him blankly.

"Don't worry, they'll tell you. And… you aren't laughing."

His discomfort is so genuine that I crack a smile. "Don't worry. I'll have the pasta. Steakhouses keep it on the menu to save dudes like you from first date fiascos… N-not t-that I think we're on a date."

"Imagine that." Richard chuckles. "I'd be sweating cold right now. So why the meat aversion?"

"Do you really care?"

"Is it a sensitive subject?"

"Not for me, but sometimes people get defensive-aggressive about their right to eat meat."

"I won't bite, I promise."

He meant it as a joke, but the phrase only makes me imagine the touch of Richard's lips on my neck as his teeth graze my skin. *Brrrrrrrrrrrrrrr*. I forcibly pull my degenerate brain away from neck-biting scenarios and back to meat-avoiding diets.

"Well, there's the animal cruelty, of course," I say. "The fact that meat is actually bad for our health. And the staggering amount of pollution and water consumption it takes to feed, grow, and slaughter a cow."

Richard is looking at me with a weird expression, his lips contracted and eyebrows drawn together. I'm not sure if he's embarrassed, or if he's trying too hard not to laugh. The latter, I suspect.

He clears his throat before speaking. "Is it just meat or everything coming from animals you don't eat?"

"I'm vegetarian, not vegan. Otherwise, you'd be totally screwed as I wouldn't eat a thing in this place. Anyway, I try to steer clear of dairy, but I eat eggs if they come from happy chickens."

Richard's lips twitch. "And how do you assess the happiness of chickens?"

"If they're free-range chickens that eat real grass and are not stuck in a cage all their lives, they're happy chickens."

The boss roars with laughter. "I'm sorry," he says between chuckles. "But before today, the welfare of chickens was a foreign concept." Still smirking, he adds, "And I don't mean it in an insensitive way."

The server arrives with our salads.

Richard takes a forkful of his bacon-covered lettuce wedge and asks, "So you're never having a bite of meat ever again in your life?"

I take a second before answering. *Never eat meat* is part of the list, but so is *never make exceptions*. I'll make the exception to stay a vegetarian and cross out the two.

"Nope."

After the potentially rocky introduction, the conversation flows between us for the entire evening. Our food arrives—T-bone for him, mushroom fettuccini for me—and we eat, drink wine, and chat happily.

"So how was it growing up in England?" I ask at one point. "Did you do all that cool Harry Potter stuff?"

Richard stops cutting his steak. "You mean battling the most powerful dark wizard of all time and destroying his soul bit by bit?"

"No." I giggle. "I meant going to a fancy boarding school in a castle somewhere with houses and everything…"

"Ah, that part. Then, yes. I told you boarding school is where I met Chris."

"Was it as cool as Hogwarts?"

"If you can compare math to charms and chemistry to potions…"

"I guess being away from your parents was a plus too."

The boss frowns. "Not really. Okay, being away from home was an adventure at thirteen, but I missed the old folks."

"I would've given everything to leave home at thirteen instead of having to wait five extra years."

"Why?"

I hesitate. "Well, my parents' marriage wasn't exactly a

happy one…"

"They argued a lot?"

"No, more… politely ignored each other. And they were so strict with me. Don't do this, don't do that…"

Richard smiles. "Now I'm beginning to understand that list of yours."

I drop my fork and cover my face with both hands. "I still can't believe you read the list. I try to forget about it."

"Besides getting drunk and arrested, how's the conquering going?"

Liquid courage, help me. In one gulp, I finish the wine in my glass and Richard pours me another one. "I bet I could still win at Never Have I Ever."

He throws me an interrogative stare.

"The drinking game?"

The boss shakes his head. "How does it work?"

"All participants take turns in saying something embarrassing or daring they've never done. All others who've done that particular deed have to drink a shot. I never took a shot."

"So your new life's goal is to get wasted at a drinking game?"

No, apparently it's digging my own conversational grave. "Of course not. I'm just saying that if I were to play, I'd still end up sober because I've done nothing that interesting."

"Besides getting arrested."

"I wouldn't call that interesting." I need to change the subject, *fast*. "But enough about me, tell me more about England."

That gets him started on boarding school, his college years, and eventually the move to the big city. Richard is in the middle of telling me how much he loves London when I ask the wrong question.

"So why base Inceptor in New York?"

The boss shakes his head and looks far away into another life, mouth tense, lips pressed in a sad line. The easy-going atmosphere drains away from the table, only to be replaced by a thick emotional wall between us.

Richard stares at his plate and takes a sip of wine. "Something happened, and I needed a change of scenery."

He doesn't look at me as he speaks, and I don't know what to do. I'd like to ask more, but I sense it'd be an awful idea. Especially with him sending me mind-your-own-business vibes so strong I'm tempted to run to the restroom and hide there. *Hello, brain? Please provide something to say.* But I was never good at improvising.

Richard proves better. "How was your pasta?" he asks.

"The fettuccini were delicious," I say, glad he came up with a conversational decoy.

"Good."

There's a weird, too-intense look in his eyes. Surely, fettuccini—tasty as they are—can't make the boss this emotional.

"What?" I ask.

"I'm just glad you don't eat burgers."

That's a weird thing to say. "Why?"

He shakes his head again in that resigned way. "It's a long story."

Uh-oh. Was the ex a meat-eater? A burgers-lover? She must've been.

"It's getting late," Richard says, shifting the topic completely. "We should probably ask for the bill."

No sooner has the word bill left Richard's lips that our server magically appears next to us. *Is the table bugged?*

"Would you care to have that boxed, sir?"

Richard and I reply at the same time.

Him: "No, thank you."

Me: "Yes, please."

The server stares at us, confused.

"We'll take everything," I say. "Please box the bread as well."

The server boxes our leftovers and hands me the bag. "Can I get you anything else? Coffee? A dessert?"

"Just the bill," Richard says.

The server takes it out of his apron and drops it on the table. "Please take as much time as you like."

Richard slips some dollar bills into the leather folder and gets up. I follow.

"I thought you didn't eat meat," he says, jerking his chin toward the doggy bag in my hands.

"No, but since the poor beast has already been slaughtered, I'd like to put the sacrifice to good use."

Near the low wall separating the beach from the promenade, a homeless man is sitting on the floor with his back against the barrier. Balancing my tight dress and spiky heels, I crouch in front of him, feeling Richard's gaze burning a hole in my back.

I give the food to the poor man and try to ignore the filth on his hands as he shakes mine to thank me. Trying not to fall on my butt, I straighten up and turn around ready to be taunted.

"Go ahead," I say. "Call me goody two-shoes all you like." The remark has stayed with me since he bailed me out of prison.

Richard gives me a long stare. "I wasn't going to."

Something in his gaze makes it impossible for me to keep eye contact, so I walk away.

Richard falls into step next to me. "That was very generous. Such a simple way to help, but the thought never even crossed my mind."

I look at him, searching his eyes for any trace of mockery. There's none.

"These people... it's so easy for them to disappear. We

become so used to seeing them on the streets that they become invisible, but they each have their stories. You'd be surprised by some."

"You know many homeless?"

"In a way. I volunteer at my neighborhood canteen for the poor once a month. When I have time, I sit down for a chat."

"That's remarkable. You're putting me to shame."

"A day a month is nothing. I bet you did more good with your donation for tomorrow night."

"Maybe, but that's just money. Devoting your time to a good cause is different. Come here, Walker"—Richard slips an arm around my shoulders—"let's go get some sleep."

Together? I don't think he meant it like that. *Pity.* Anyway, it's the first time he's called me by my last name—I like it—or touched me beyond a handshake. I'm not sure if it's a gesture of camaraderie or… something else. I let my shoulders enjoy the weight of Richard's arm and try not to read too much into it.

At the hotel, we stand awkwardly in front of my door to say good night. I-had-two-glasses-of-wine me wants to haul Richard into my room and onto the bed by the collar of his shirt, but it would probably require I-had-two-bottles-of-wine me to do something like that. So I politely say good night and agree to meet him in the morning for a day of sightseeing. I slip under the covers, alone, feeling a disproportionate euphoria at the idea of touring LA with the boss.

Indira was right; I'm in so much trouble.

Eleven

Never Skinny Dip

Thanks to the three-hour jet lag, I'm up earlier than usual at four thirty. Even if it's seven thirty in New York, I doubt Nikki will be up, unless Chevron—tuned to my hours—dragged her off the bed. Either way, better if I wait a couple more hours before I call. It's silly how quickly I've turned into such an anxious pet parent, but I literally feel like I've left my child behind.

I change into running gear—leggings, tank top, iPod strap, fit watch—and wander down to the lobby.

"Hi," I say, startling a half-asleep receptionist.

"Hello, ma'am." He jerks himself awake and sits straighter in his chair. "How may I help you?"

"Is there a good running trail around here?"

The clerk blinks at me, still shocked someone would be this chirpy at such an ungodly hour. But he recovers fast. "Er, the best option would be to turn left as soon as you exit the hotel and run along the beach. If you head south, you'll find yourself on the Strand, a paved bike path that will bring you to the Venice boardwalk. Or you could go north and loop Palisades Park."

"Is the park open this early?"

"Yeah, it's twenty-four hours."

"Great, thanks."

I press play on the iPod and jog outside where it's still entirely dark. There's only a hint of light glimmering behind the hills on my right, which means the temperature is still manageable. I doubt I'd be able to run with the Californian sun shining high in the sky.

I turn left, follow the road to the beach trail, and head north toward the park. If the Hudson waterfront is one my favorite trails in New York, it has nothing on the ocean. I'm only missing Chevron.

After the first loop, I check my watch. *Eight minutes per mile.* Way below my average. Lately, I've only had time to run on the weekends, and my lack of constant training is showing. I should start over, but I'm too lazy, so from the park, I cross over a bridge to the beach to go exploring. The shore is deserted, too dark even for surfers.

As I stare at the water, a terrible idea strikes me. Faster than I can stop myself, I remove all my clothes and run into the ocean stark naked. *Never skinny dip—I can cross you off the list!*

I don't linger in the cool water more than thirty seconds. Not just because I'm butt naked in a public space, but also because the Pacific is freezing. I re-dress faster than ever and with fresh adrenaline pumping in my bloodstream, I run back to the hotel, breaking every personal speed record ever made.

By seven, I'm showered, dressed, and ready to rock LA. I'm finishing applying makeup when a knock distracts me.

"Who is it?" I call.

"Richard."

My stomach does a triple axel. I slip on my cord wedges—a good compromise between the necessity to wear heels and a long day of walking—and open the door.

"Whoa." Richard's eyes widen. "And I thought I was up early," he says, eyeing my already-prim attire.

He's still wearing gray sweatpants and a black T-shirt. Soft, damp curls are clinging to his forehead as if he just came out of the shower, which he must have. *Someone, please shoot me now!* Sweat-panted Richard is too good a sight, and showering Richard too good a fantasy, for me to preserve my brain cells.

"I'm a morning person," I say apologetically. "And there's

the jet lag."

"Yeah, so would it be okay to meet downstairs in fifteen?"

"Super, see yah there."

***

Richard jerks his chin toward my shoes, unimpressed. "Are you sure you want to walk in those all day?"

So wedges aren't his thing. Mmm, I'll see if I can do better tonight.

"Yeah, I always wear heels."

"Why?"

We are not all blessed with Saskia Landon's legs.

"I just love heels."

"But we'll be walking a lot."

"I'm used to it, no big deal."

He shrugs. "I was thinking we should turn today into something different." *Thu-thump, thu-thump, thu-thump. Can anyone else hear my heart beating?* "Would your readers be interested in an 'LA in One Day' feature?"

Good thing I removed the fit watch. Otherwise, it'd be sending off all kinds of alarms at my heart stopping to beat due to mortification. When will my brain finally grasp that this is only work for Richard? Strictly business. No romantic agenda.

"You might've just dug your own grave." I smirk vindictively.

"Why?"

"Because my readership would prefer something titled 'One Day Shopping Spree in LA.'"

"Ah. You're killing me." Richard mockingly brings a hand to his chest. "Where should we start?"

"A walk towards the unique finds of Venice Beach, and then we'll work our way up to Rodeo Drive."

***

Richard bears the window-shopping like a man. From Venice to Beverly Hills to the Fashion District, he follows me around town not once complaining. I select a bunch of indie stores and interview the owners and designers. Richard is a good sport even when we try out a few male boutiques, going so far as to offer himself up as a human guinea pig—er, *male model.*

As we walk out of the umpteenth shop, Richard asks, "How much time do you need to get ready for tonight?"

"An hour, an hour and a half tops. Why? Should we already head back?"

Richard looks at his watch and sighs. "No, we're good for another two hours or so."

"Then what do you say we do something non-shopping related?"

The relief on his face is humorous.

"What did you have in mind?"

"A quick trip to Griffith Observatory. Everyone agrees it's the one view in LA you can't miss."

"Will we have time? With traffic and everything."

I check my phone. "The map app authority says it's half an hour to get there and half an hour to get back to Santa Monica, even in traffic."

"And how long from Santa Monica to downtown?"

I swap addresses. "Half an hour."

Everything seems to be spaced half an hour away in LA.

"Then we're good."

Richard calls an Uber, and we ask the driver to wait for us as we do a quick tour of the observatory.

After taking a couple—okay, an unhealthy number—of pictures of the Hollywood sign, we make our way along the promenade that wraps around the main dome. We stop under an arch to admire the Los Angeles skyline. The day is clear, and the view stretches far into the distance.

"This city is ginormous," I say. "I could never live here."

"Because of the long drives?"

"No, the weather. Too hot."

"I thought you'd enjoy the warmth."

"Why?"

"You're like fire."

I stare up at him and find him gazing intensely at me.

"Let me guess, the hair? I get that a lot."

"Yeah." He nods, looking almost relieved. "The hair."

Being this close to Richard, his scent fills my nostrils. *Pine cones and rain.* Even in sunny California, the boss still manages to smell like a cold winter day.

"Anyway, I prefer winter…" and before I can shut my stupid mouth, I blab the next thought that pops into my head, "Your aftershave smells like a snowy forest, you know?"

No time to add anything to justify my silly, and totally inappropriate comment before his jaw tightens and his eyes harden.

"We should probably go," Richard says, looking away. "The meter is running."

"Sure."

I follow him around the dome and back to the car with a large, inexplicable lump in my throat.

***

The wistfulness of the observatory visit dissipates as I take advantage of every minute I have to get ready. I scrub and pamper myself until I'm the best beauty products can make me. Tablet connected to the hotel Wi-Fi, I experiment with two of Tracy's tutorials to style my hair in a loose hairdo, and contour my cheekbones so they'd make Katharine Hepburn burn with shame.

At the designated hour, I make my way down to the lobby and, for once, Richard's eyes don't wander straight to my shoes but linger on my plunging neckline. I take a deep breath and try not to blush.

"Wow." Richard's eyes widen. "You're stunning."

"Don't sound so surprised," I say.

"No, it's just... I didn't expect your dress to be so..." Flattering? Revealing? Sexy? I'm right there with you, Richard, I would've never expected to wear a dress like this, not in a million years. *"...colorful."*

"Colorful?" That's not the adjective I was expecting.

"Yeah, somehow I had myself convinced you'd come out in a black dress."

Which I totally would have if it weren't for the stupid list and stupid friends. "Why black?"

"It's safe."

"Are you calling me boring?" I say, more flirtatious than reproachful.

My coquettishness earns me a smile, a real one, not Richard's usual guarded smirk. And as the boss lets himself go, his entire face changes. Crinkly lines appear at the corners of his eyes, and for once, warmth radiates from his gaze instead of mistrust. His sexy dimples make an appearance too. If I thought he was handsome before, I knew nothing. When Richard smiles, really smiles, he is sensational. It sucks the air out of my lungs and sends my heart into a pounding frenzy.

"I wouldn't dare," he says.

"You clean up well yourself," I manage to say.

"Shall we go?"

He offers me his arm and I take it. Outside, we hop in a cab and spend the obligatory half-hour journey mostly in silence. I am too self-conscious of my spiraling crush to make small talk. Like an inexperienced teenager, I jolt in my seat every time our legs bump due to a sharp turn.

After stepping out of the cab, we're admitted to the red carpet by security. I'm blinded by the photographers' flashes and their reflections on the metallic walls of the Disney Concert Hall. The paps, however, soon realize we're nobodies, and the clicking craze stops.

At the end of the carpet, there's a small press area with other correspondents from magazines and TV. We're early. The big celebrities will start arriving a bit later. Presumably in a slow trickle that will carry on for at least an hour. Events managers time the arrivals so that all the guests will get their dedicated moment in front of the photographers and with the press.

"I should wait here," I tell Richard. "See who gets in, do some interviews…"

"I'll get started on the champagne." He winks at me and disappears inside.

Alone and with work to do, I regain some presence of mind—meaning only half of my brain cells are being fried by the memory of Richard's smile.

Plus, red carpets are fun! All the celebrities I meet are incredibly down-to-earth and exciting to talk to. They make jokes, tell me wardrobe malfunction anecdotes, and I record more than a few good quotes to publish in a bubbly article on the evening. Even if I'm from a relatively unknown magazine, no one snubs me. And the first part of the night flies by in a series of incredible conversations, swooshing gowns, and some fan-girl moments on my part. When no one new arrives for twenty minutes, I move inside to finally join the real party.

I queue with some other guests at the wardrobe. Nothing can

be brought upstairs. Phones, bags, jackets… everything has to be checked in.

I've just dropped my clutch when I find myself face to face—more face to chin—with my nemesis: Aurora Vanderbilt.

Aurora's lips part in an evil smirk as she says, "Blair, good to see you. I didn't know amateurs were invited."

We haven't seen each other since she stole my promotion, so my reply is pure vitriol. "You mean you thought it was a party reserved for toddlers still attached to their mother's skirts?"

As if on cue, Rebecca Vanderbilt appears at her daughter's side. "Who's your friend, dear?" she asks.

Aurora gives me a look of death. "No one," she says, steering her mother away.

Blood pulsing, I let them go and wait at a distance for the next elevator. Aurora being here isn't the only reason I'm edgy. Richard is waiting for me upstairs. In the last hour, I've met and spoken to a good chunk of the sexiest men alive top-ten chart, but no one gave me goose bumps the way only thinking about Richard does.

If my Belle-goes-to-the-ball dreamy filters weren't set high enough already, the event being hosted at Disney Hall's rooftop garden doesn't help. Talk about enchanting venues. Up here, it's all blooming trees and winding pathways around a magical rose fountain, all enclosed by sweeping metallic walls. As romantic settings go, it doesn't get any more suggestive than this space.

I step out of the elevator and walk into this wonderland of fairy lights and whimsical alleys accompanied by Disney-esque classical music playing in the background. To ease the anxiety gnawing at my stomach, I grab a few canapés and wash them down with champagne.

"There you are."

Richard's voice makes me jump so high that if my glass were

still full, I would've splashed us both with bubbly.

"Richard." I turn, steadying myself.

In the semi-darkness, his sharp features appear even more attractive, aided by flickering shadows and contrast. Maybe it's just the tux. That must be it. You can *so* judge a book by its cover. I'm judging right now. More than judging, I'm thinking of ripping the cover off the book entirely.

"Did you have a good time downstairs?"

"Yeah, wonderful. I collected loads of material." I smile tensely. "Don't worry, I'll be able to put together a few amazing editorials."

"I'm not worried. I've complete confidence in your work."

Someone bumps into him from behind, and Richard stumbles forward, landing with both hands on my bare collarbones. Whoa! I'm being electrocuted. Tingling electric currents spread from my shoulders down my arms and up my neck to my brain where the last few surviving cells are being short-circuited for good.

Richard steadies himself but doesn't pull away immediately. We stand there, under a tree blossoming with ridiculously pretty red flowers, staring into each other's eyes. Finally, Richard frowns and takes a step back. Neither of us speaks, and the silence becomes awkward quickly. A server breaks it by offering us a tray of hors d'oeuvre. Richard declines, but I take one and stuff my mouth full before I say something stupid.

Panic swells as I'm about to swallow the last bite. Richard hasn't taken his eyes off me and still isn't speaking. What am I going to say when I've finished chewing and have no more excuses to keep quiet? Will we just stay here all evening, staring at each other in utter silence?

My dilemma is solved by some six-foot-four hulking human careening into Richard and pulling him into a bear hug. "Mate, you're here."

Richard and the newcomer start a primordial dance of friendly grunts and shoulders slaps. When the ritual is over, the stranger turns, and I'm blinded by Hollywood's most wanted million-dollar smile.

"Blair, this is my good friend Christian," Richard makes the introductions. "Chris meet Blair."

"Hi," I say, and shake Christian Slade's hand as if I was used to meeting out-of-this-world-gorgeous men all the time.

A tiny part of me wants to take a selfie with him and post it on my Instagram feed right away. So I'm equally disappointed and relieved that only the official event photographer is admitted up here. At least I'm forced not to embarrass myself with the request, but I want the selfie so badly.

Richard and "Chris" do some catching up, and I'm content to just ogle the pair. It's like staring at a box of bonbons, trying to decide which one you want to eat first. These two are the yin and yang of masculine sex appeal. Christian: tall, blonde, green-eyed. Richard: equally tall, dark hair, dark eyes. Both impossibly sexy. Both with knee-wobble-inducing British accents. And both bachelors. *Yum!*

"So, how's the evening going?" Richard asks Christian after a while.

"Ah, too much public relations. I need a break." That's when the mega-Hollywood star surprises me bending his head toward me in a small bow. "May I steal the lady for a dance?"

Twelve

Never Make the First Move

Aaaaaaaah! Christian Slade, asking me to dance?!

"Sure," I say, taking his hand.

There's a small square in the garden serving as a dance floor, and some other couples are already swaying in the middle. Christian escorts me to the center, and we start swirling in time with the music. With a hand on my lower back and the other holding mine, he leads me like a professional.

"You're an impressive dancer," I say.

"You seem surprised."

"Not many men can waltz this gracefully, not in this century at least."

He chuckles. "Comes with the job, I guess."

"Of being an actor?"

"Yeah, sooner or later we all have to star in a costume movie with a ball, and the dance-like-a-gentleman training becomes mandatory."

"What movie?"

Christian raises a brow. "Not a fan, I take it?"

I blush. "No, it's not that. But I'm not a stalker either. You've been in so many movies… I don't remember them all."

"Which ones have you seen, then?"

"Ah, well. Last year's sci-fi flick… mmm… *Dancing in the Rain,* of course. See, that's another one you had to waltz in."

"Indeed. That's my excuse for being a good dancer—what's yours?"

"Several years of ballet with some ballroom dancing on the side."

"Brilliant."

"Your real-life British accent sounds weird."

Christian flashes me another of his million-dollar smiles. "You don't like it?"

"No, I do. It's just that on TV, you usually speak American. It's fascinating how you can sound totally natural with both accents."

Christian chuckles. "That's diction training for you. And having an American mum helped too." He winks.

Is he flirting? Wow, it's so weird to dance with a man I've only seen on TV who's so incredibly gorgeous. Mr. Slade here looks like a marble statue, and I'm pretty sure his skin is smoother than mine. Not to mention, Christian has been named "Sexiest Man Alive" three years in a row, as well as Hollywood's most wanted bachelor. This whole experience is surreal.

But for all his good looks and A-list status, I'm still at ease talking to him. And, weirdly enough, I don't want to rip his clothes off and haul him off to my hotel room. Chatting with him feels more like talking to an old friend.

"You have an odd expression," Christian says, interrupting my musings.

"It's just that you're so normal." That came out wrong. He raises his brows and I hurry to explain better. "I thought I'd be completely star-struck by you. But you're just a regular human being."

Christian is silent for a split second, making me worry I might've offended him. But then he throws back his head, roaring with laughter.

My cheeks heat up. "Did I say something wrong?"

"No," Christian says, still chuckling. "I wish I met more people like you."

The song changes and we pause for a second.

"Another round?" Christian asks.

"Sure," I say, and let him pirouette me around.

After some more dancing, I ask, "Do people treat you very differently?"

"You've no idea. Feeling normal is a welcome novelty."

"Aren't actors supposed to have these huge egos? You know, always needing to be the center of attention."

"Not *all* the time, makes me wish I had a switch. Of course, it's cool to meet fans and have people ask for autographs and pictures, but sometimes it's exhausting to catch the awe in people's eyes. It makes building real relationships hard."

"Is that why you're still single?"

Christian frowns, and his movements become more rigid. "Am I off the record?"

"Completely, t-totally off the record," I stutter. "I'm so sorry. Did I give you the impression I was interviewing you?"

"My fault." He shakes his head, and his hand relaxes again in mine. "But it has happened before. I say something in a friendly conversation and the next day my words get printed on page one."

"That must suck."

"It does. It's made me suspicious of even the most innocent questions. And yes, it makes it almost impossible to date."

"Why?"

"Every time I meet someone who's not *Hollywood*," he rolls his eyes as if to air-quote the word Hollywood. "I wonder if the girl likes me only for the fame, money, or worse if she's in love with one of my characters…"

I smirk. "I'm sure uncanny good looks are a factor too."

Christian chuckles again. "See, no one ever gives me cheek."

"So why don't you date fellow celebrities? Actresses must

be immune to the fame thing."

"Ah, see, but they're not. In a way, it's even worse."

Another song goes by, and we only nod to each other and keep dancing.

"Why are actresses worse than fans?"

"The movie industry is weird, complicated and... layered. It sort of has hierarchies."

"I'm sure you can date out of your caste, though."

Before replying, Christian spins me in an inside-outside turn. "Sure I can. But when I date someone less famous, I can't help wondering if she likes *me* or the career boost and extra publicity in gossip magazines. It's a feeling I can't shake. And if I were to date someone more famous, then she'd probably have the same doubts. Not to mention that dating actresses is a nightmare. Schedules are the worst. Most of my past breakups happened due to scheduling conflicts."

"You sound as wretched as Julia Roberts in *Notting Hill* when she tries to get the last brownie."

As another song ends, Christian lifts me up and smiles as he lowers me down. "I'm just saying it's not all bling."

I squeeze his hand and motion him to pick up the quicker rhythm of the new song.

"So basically," I say. "You need to meet a girl who's never watched a day of TV in her life, fall in love with her, and make her fall for you."

"And how many girls like that do you know?"

Countless nights spent binge-watching TV shows with Nikki flash before my eyes. "Not many, I agree."

"Blair, you're an amusing little thing. Where has Richard been hiding you?"

I turn rigid in his arms.

Christian immediately notices my discomfort. "What did I

say wrong?"

"I'm self-conscious about my height, or lack of thereof," I say, which isn't a lie, but also isn't the truth. Just hearing Richard's name turns me into a bundle of nerves.

"Really? Don't be. Men love tiny women."

"And of the many adjectives women enjoy, 'tiny' and 'little' are not on the list."

"Petite?"

"Nope."

"Mmm, delicate?"

I raise my eyebrows.

"Okay, I'll drop it."

"Sage man."

"What about you?" Christian goes back to our original conversation. "Any man in your life?"

I shake my head.

"I know I'm not supposed to ask, but how come?"

"Well, I spent my life giving too much importance to stupid things and wasted the last three years on a cheating bastard. So right now I'm focusing on myself and on straightening my priorities."

And on the side, I have this ridiculous crush on my boss, you know, your friend Richard—the one who doesn't do relationships.

"How's that going?" Christian asks.

"So far, I changed jobs, my ex threatened to sue me on multiple occasions… mmm… I experienced my first hangover, got arrested, and adopted a stray dog."

Christian laughs wholeheartedly, then lets out a low whistle. "And I thought my life was interesting. What did you do to get arrested?"

The music slows to an end again. How many songs have we

danced together? I've lost count. I'm about to answer Christian's question and launch into another dance when a towering presence appears next to us.

Richard has a weird expression on his face. Hard to say what's going on inside his head, but he seems annoyed.

"If you dance another song together," the boss says, looking at me, "you'll end up on all the gossip magazine covers as Christian Slade's mysterious new flame."

"Richard, mate." Christian lets me go and takes a step back. "I've been selfish; I completely stole your date."

"Blair isn't my date, she's here to report."

Since Richard asked me to join him on this Californian weekend, a tiny hope has been burning inside me. Hope that these few days together away from the office mean more than a business trip. Hope that something will happen between us, that if something in New York is impossible... you know, what happens in Hollywood stays in Hollywood.

Richard's words extinguish that hope completely. They chill my heart and fill my mouth with the taste of ashes.

Christian smiles, shaking his head. "Mate, you're such a slave worker." He pats Richard on the shoulder and then looks at me. "Group projects back in school were the same. Richard kept us all in line."

I try to smile, and I hope the tight-lipped grimace I'm producing doesn't look as ashen as my heart feels.

"I've got to mingle with the other guests anyway," Christian adds. "Blair, it's been a pleasure." He takes my hand and kisses it. "You'll tell me all about your adventures next time."

I manage to nod. Christian pats Richard on the shoulder one more time and is gone.

Refusing to meet Richard's eye, I say, "I was tired of dancing, anyway." I make to shuffle away from the dance floor.

"Not so quickly."

Richard grabs me by the waist and pulls our bodies together while imprisoning my left hand in his. Without another word, he leads me back to the center of the square to dance.

The boss's style is more basic, a steady one, two, three... one, two, three... But honestly, I couldn't care less about Richard's dancing skills, not when he's looking at me as he is now.

I'm confused. He just spelled out for everyone that this isn't a date. I mean, if this is the way Richard stares at his non-dates, how much neuro-damage can he inflict on his date-dates?

As we dance, neither of us talks. We just move, staring into each other eyes. It's some sort of non-verbal conversation that is making my head spin like no pirouette ever did. I get lost in the brown of Richard's eyes, and the world around us disappears. Only our bodies exist. The heat of his right hand on my lower back, the pressure of his hand on mine as he holds it, and his hypnotizing gaze.

I don't know how long we dance, or for how many songs, or to what rhythm and steps. I notice only when the music stops. Someone, somewhere, is making a speech, probably Christian. I don't care. I only care that Richard has let go of my hand and I've been suddenly deprived of his body heat.

The boss takes a step back, looking at me as if I was a murder scene.

Still looking horrified, Richard shakes his head once and backs further away. Before I can say or do anything, he's making a run for it.

What the hell was that?

I try to chase after him, but my gown isn't exactly conducive to running. The full skirt certainly doesn't help me navigate the crowd converging toward the center of the garden to listen to

Christian's speech.

Slowly, elbowing my way through Hollywood's best, I manage to reach the edge of the group. Richard is nowhere to be seen. I frantically turn my head left and right, but he's not here. Not caring that it's rude to leave without saying goodbye to the host, I take the elevators down and walk to the wardrobe to retrieve my shawl and clutch.

My phone is in my hands as soon as the clerk hands me the clutch. I try Richard's number... straight to voicemail. From upstairs comes a boom of applause and, slowly, all the guests start spilling out of the elevators and walking through the reception hall toward me. Well, toward their coats more accurately. Before the horde can trap me, I hurry outside. On the steps of Disney Hall, I try his number again and... get his voicemail again. *Awesome.* Richard has fried my brain with his insane eyes and made every fiber of my body want him even more, and now he's disappeared.

Something boils in my veins. I'm not sure if it's fury or lust, but I'm certain I'm not ready to let this go. He can't dance with me like that and then leave me here to fend for myself. *Sorry, Richard, but I know where you're sleeping tonight.* I hail a cab and give the driver the hotel address.

***

In the lobby, I pause at the reception desk. There's a line, so I wait my turn impatiently tapping a shoe on the marble floor. The receptionist is a statuesque blonde who must go around LA carrying headshots. Around here, it seems every other person is in their job only temporarily, waiting to make their big break as actors.

"How can I help you, ma'am?" the receptionist finally asks me.

"I'm traveling with Mr. Richard Stratton. He's staying in room 354. We got separated at a charity gala and his phone must've died." The receptionist keeps on a kind expression, but she's probably wondering why I'm telling her the story of my life. *TMI, Blair.* "Anyway, I just wanted to check if Mr. Stratton came back."

"Very well, I can call his room for you." The receptionist focuses on the screen in front of her, clicks the mouse twice, and then looks back at me. "I'm sorry, ma'am, but Mr. Stratton has activated the 'do not disturb' function. We cannot contact him at this time."

"Oh. Does that mean he's back?"

"The option can only be activated from within the room. So, yes, Mr. Stratton must be in his room."

"Thanks so much."

Dread and elation play a boxing match in my guts as I backtrack to the elevator. The fight continues all the way up to the eleventh floor, and by the time I get there dread wins, so I decide to stop in my room first to rally.

Down the hall, a red light next to Richard's door catches my attention. The words 'do not disturb' are spelled clearly underneath the glowing light. Is he sending me a message?

In my room, I pace, trying to decide my next move. Should I really go knock on Richard's door? *To say what?* Should I go to bed instead? *I wouldn't sleep.* The memory of dancing with Richard is too intoxicating. The feel of his hand clasping mine, his arm around my waist, our bodies pressed together... and his eyes. Oh gosh, even thinking about his stare makes me flush.

I open the window to let some air in, but it's not the cooling breeze one could expect in New York. *Stupid LA heat.* This isn't me. I'm losing my sanity, and I'm not one to lose her head over a guy—especially arrogant, meat-eating, playboy types. I'm also not one to get arrested, adopt a pet, or wear a scandalous dress. This line of thinking suited the old, list abiding me. The new me doesn't play by the rules.

On impulse, I walk toward the luggage rack, open my suitcase and fish inside for the list. The sorry sheet of paper has never been more crumpled. I lay it out on the desk, trying to flatten the edges with my palms. Pen in hand, I sit at the room's desk and scan the list. After crossing out *never make exceptions* and *never skinny dip,* I search for something that will give me an excuse to ignore Richard's 'do not disturb' sign.

There. *Never make the first move.* If ever there was a time to ignore that rule, tonight is it.

I kiss the list and get up, trying to smooth the wrinkles in my skirt. Should I change into something less dramatic? A mental vision of Richard undoing my zipper flashes through my head. His hand slowly pulling it down as he stands behind me, his breath hot on my neck. I can almost feel Richard's hands pulling down the straps of the dress over my shoulders and this once-in-a-lifetime gown falling to the floor, pooling at my feet in silky waves. *The dress stays.*

Mirror check: makeup still good, but the hair would be sexier loose. I remove all the clips and fluff it, letting the locks cascade down my back. The bobby pins have left it wavy and voluminous and the curls add a bit of wildness to my look. I give myself a wink in the mirror, and go.

Richard's room is only three doors down from mine. Standing here, I suddenly don't feel so brave. The gold metal plate with the number 354 engraved in black seems to get bigger as I stare at it. This was stupid. *Blair, go back to your room.* I take a step back; then stop. No, I'm not going back.

Inhale, exhale, and knock.

With a pounding heart, I wait for the door to open.

Thirteen
Never Lie

It takes me a few seconds to focus on the person standing in front of me. A tall woman who's looking back into the room, showing me only a mane of black hair. "Don't worry, I'm sure it's room service," she says, then turns to face me. Her mouth forms an "O" of surprise before her lips spread in a vicious smile.

"Blair, what an unexpected visit," Aurora Vanderbilt says.

Not her.

Everything within me breaks. I blink back tears of rage and frustration, but there's no fighting the angry blush that spreads across my face. The shock and misery must show along with the rash because Aurora's smile widens.

"Did you need something?" she asks in a honeyed tone.

"N-no… just work stuff… n-nothing important…"

I'm still blabbing nonsense when Richard appears on the threshold. Jacket off. Bow tie gone. Shirt invitingly open at the neck. *Sexy as hell.* Our eyes meet and a bolt of shame strikes me.

"Blair!" His eyebrows raise. "What are you doing here?"

I can't hide my disappointment, so I look away. Either he's a better actor than Christian Slade, or the electricity of the night was all inside my head. *It wasn't all inside my head.*

"N-nothing." I flutter my hands in the air. "It can wait until tomorrow."

"Are you sure?" Now his expression is closer to pity.

Mercifully, at that moment a server pushing a cart stops next to me and asks, "Is the champagne for this room?"

"Yes," Aurora says, opening the door wider.

The waiter pushes the cart inside and I seize the opportunity to escape. "I'll leave you to your... uh... thing." *Why can't I stop my hands from fluttering?* "Good night."

I don't wait for a reply. All I can say for myself is that I manage not to run. I retrace my steps to my room, insert the card in its slot with trembling hands, and rush inside. Resting my back against the door, I take a few deep breaths that quickly turn into heavy sobs.

How could I be so stupid? How could I misread the signals so badly?

I thought Richard and I had shared a moment, but clearly, all the boss cares about is sharing a bed with Aurora Vanderbilt. But I'm not crazy. Sparks happened, and it must've scared the boss so much he wanted to kill this new connection in cold blood.

Maybe.

No matter how much I try to rationalize Richard's behavior, it still sucks. And no justification will change the fact that he's spending the night in a hotel room with Aurora Vanderbilt. True, I'm not his girlfriend so it's not like he's cheating on me.

Feels that way all the same.

A glob of bile rises to my throat. I might throw up. In the bathroom, I splash my face with fresh water, not caring that it'll send the makeup streaming down my cheeks. I dry my hands and unzip the dress on my own. So much for the sexy fantasies. When the gown reaches the ground, I kick it away from my legs, abandoning it in a puddle on the bathroom floor. Back in the main room, I fling myself onto the bed and cry into a pillow until I fall asleep.

***

I wake up early after a restless night spent tossing and turning over nightmares of Aurora and Richard rolling in bed. A mix of all the fantasies I've had about Richard played before my eyes. Only the woman in the dream—*nightmare*—wasn't me.

I throw the blankets away, and after carefully washing my face, I launch myself into my running ritual. Energizing playlist, on. Fit watch, on. I-can-run-my-sorrow-to-death plan, so on.

This time I choose the running path heading south, and it doesn't take me long to reach the Venice boardwalk. With only surfers braving the waters, the beach is almost deserted this early in the morning. The quietness helps calm my nerves. So do the exercise endorphins.

I kick my shoes off and abandon the concrete trail. The sand is cool under my feet, a nice sensation after a long run. I choose a spot on a small dune to sit and stare at the ocean and the surfers paddling on the water. They seem so free and careless as they ride the waves.

When the sun starts burning my skin, I head back to the hotel. Unfortunately, the jog hasn't cleared my head as much as I'd hoped. And nothing can change the fact that I have to spend six hours stuck on a plane next to Richard.

The boss doesn't know why you knocked on his door last night.

Maybe not. Aurora might've guessed, but no one knows for sure. What if Richard asks me point-blank? A resolution forms in my heart. If asked, I'll lie through my teeth.

Hoping to work my body to exhaustion so that I'll sleep on the plane and avoid unpleasant conversation, I take the stairs up to the eleventh floor. When I get there, I'm positively puffing.

To my horror, as soon as I push the stairs door open, I spot Aurora and Richard embracing in the hallway. I freeze. My room is past theirs. I consider running away, but Aurora catches me out of the corner of her eye and presses herself even closer to Richard in a goodbye kiss.

The kiss seems to last forever, but eventually, the leech releases her sucker. Aurora walks toward the elevator, waving at me with a nasty grin on her face. That's when Richard spots me.

No escape, then. The only way is forward.

"Morning," Richard says, as I pass him.

I ignore him and carry on along the corridor, walking on tiptoes. Richard has never seen me at my real, non-heeled shortness.

He follows me. "Hey, I'm talking to you."

"Morning."

"Would you please stop for a second?"

"Why?"

"Did you want to discuss something last night?"

"I wanted to pick your brain on some creative ideas…" I say, not looking at him and trying to fit the key in its slot. My hands are shaking so badly it's difficult.

"What ideas?"

I give up the fighting and spin around to face the boss. "It doesn't matter. I sorted everything out on my own."

"I'd like to hear those ideas all the same."

"I thought you didn't micromanage."

"Why are you being so snippy?"

The nerve of him to ask.

"I'm not. I'm sweaty and what I'd like to do is go take a shower. Last night, I wanted to discuss ideas, but you seemed more interested in trolloping. And I don't want to talk about it now."

Richard scowls. "Aurora isn't a whore."

"I wasn't talking about dear *Aurora*."

121

As soon as the words leave my mouth, I regret them. He'll catch me now, see right through me. The boss will know this is all my jealousy talking.

"Judging again, are we?" Richard's voice rises. "I'm an adult and single. I can do whatever I please."

Thank you, boss, for showing all the limitations of your male brain.

"Of course you can."

"And you can stop your self-righteous tantrum and bring that prissy ass of yours back to earth."

I narrow my eyes. "If you think this is me judging your lifestyle then you're such a brazen idiot, I feel sorry for you." And then I add what I've really been burning to say. "Or you're playing dumb, which is even worse!"

Working behind my back, I give the key another try and finally manage to slide it into the slot. In a swift move, I free the lock, enter the room, and slam the door right in his idiotic, arrogant—stupidly handsome—face.

Richard pounds his fists on the wood almost immediately. "What's that supposed to mean? Hey, open this door."

I unstrap my iPod from the belt on my arm and plug it into the dock station sitting on the nightstand. "Sorry, I can't hear you," I shout. And to make sure my statement is true, I blast the speakers until I can't actually hear the pounding anymore.

With a nod of satisfaction, I shed my sweaty clothes to the floor and hop into the shower.

***

"If you keep staring at that window like that, it'll melt," Richard says.

I scoff, shrug, and do not turn my head. I keep my arms crossed over my chest and my gaze focused on the clouds out of the plane's window.

"So you're going to pretend I don't exist for the next six hours?"

Finally, I turn. "How could you sleep with Aurora?" I hiss.

Richard raises both eyebrows. "Excuse me?"

"Of all people, why *her?*"

"Why not? Aurora is very attractive… a lot of fun."

Which I'm not, I suppose. Oh, why did I ask? His words are like daggers to the heart. Richard wants to keep pretending I've no reason to be upset?

Let's pretend along.

"She also stands for everything you hate," I point out, trying to move the conversation away from my obvious, blinding jealousy.

"What do you mean?"

"Aurora never had to work a day in her life for what she has. Mommy fed it all to her with a silver spoon."

"Oh, so that's where the drama comes from. You're jealous because she beat you for the editor position at Évoque."

Oh, Richard, if only you knew work is not an envy trigger here. Still, better than you knowing the truth.

"Aurora didn't beat me, she cheated. Her mother bought the position for her."

"So she's from a rich, privileged family and she takes advantage. Wouldn't you do the same?"

"Not if my family actually stole money by not paying taxes. How dare they show their faces at a fund-raising? They must enjoy pretending to be generous to the community while they're ripping everyone off instead. All that extra cash has to go somewhere… right?"

Richard chastises me with a reproachful expression. "That's a very serious accusation to make."

"Not an accusation, *a fact.*"

"You've proof?"

"There were rumors at Évoque about a story on Rebecca Vanderbilt that got killed before publication."

"Are we talking office gossip or real facts?"

"A rumor like that wouldn't spread for no reason."

"Why would the magazine kill the story?"

"Too serious for our type of publication and Maison Vanderbilt is a big cross-magazine advertiser at Northwestern. Even more now after they had to shop for Aurora's promotion."

"Is the reporter who had the lead interested in selling it elsewhere?"

"She can't freelance while working at Évoque. Why? I don't see you running a story about dear Aurora's mommy."

"If Rebecca Vanderbilt is cooking her books, you're damn right I want to run the story."

I finally relax my pout. "Are you serious?"

"Bring me proof and I'll publish the article."

"How am I supposed to prove anything? I'm not a reporter. I never did investigative journalism, I wouldn't know where to start. And finance isn't my strong suit."

"But you're smart, bet you can figure a way."

"For real? You're not just saying this?"

"If you can get the evidence, the story is a go."

"Deal."

We shake hands, and I regret the physical contact immediately. Richard holds my hand, and my gaze, a second longer than necessary, and I can't help but enjoy the sensation.

Arrrgh, this man will be the death of me.

***

That night I'm brooding in solitude on the couch when the apartment door opens and Nikki walks in with Chevron in tow.

"Hey, you're back." My roomie smiles. "How was Hollywood?"

"A disaster."

"That good, huh?"

"Imagine the worst thing that ever happened to you. It was worse."

Nikki releases Chevron's leash and they sit down and jump, respectively, onto the cushions next to me. "Better or worse than Bridget Jones going to the house party in the bunny costume?"

"Worse: I was humiliated."

"Better or worse than when Ross said 'we were on a break'?"

"Worse."

"Better or worse than when Jon Snow died on *Game of Thrones?*"

"Nothing could ever be worse than Jon Snow dying," I hiss.

"See? Then there's hope." She pats my knee. "Tell me what happened."

I do.

"Ah, well." Nikki sighs. "I'd still swap lives."

I make big eyes at her. "Why?"

"At least you went out and met Christian Slade. I'm married to my job and in love with my sister's boyfriend... So..."

"What a pair!"

Pale as hell and with blue bags under her eyes, Nikki does look even more downcast than me.

"What happened to you?" I ask.

Nikki stares ahead, unfocused. "I bumped into Paul."

"Was he alone?"

"Yeah."

"And?"

"We had coffee."

"And?"

"He was nice and polite as you should be with your girlfriend's sister. Every time I see him, *them…* I die a little inside."

"And Julia still has no idea?"

Nikki massages her temples and shrugs. "Sometimes I think it was obvious something was happening with Paul when she swept in and stole him. Other times I think I'm so damn introverted that maybe it was obvious only to me, and neither Julia nor Paul have any idea how I felt."

"So the 'time cures all ills' motto doesn't really work?"

"I'm afraid not. I've spent the last two years hoping my sister's love life will crumble to pieces. What does that say about me?"

"That we can be spinsters together, all three of us."

"*Woof.*"

Nikki shakes her head. "At least someone's excited at the prospective." She pats Chevron. "No, seriously, there's no hope for me, but what's your next move?"

I stare out the window at Manhattan's lights. "Grind Aurora into the ground and bring the whole Vanderbilt fashion empire down with her and her witch of a mother."

"You know Aurora Vanderbilt isn't the real problem, right?"

"What do you mean?"

"It could've been anyone else in Richard's room. It would've hurt just as much."

"No, it wouldn't."

"Okay, you hate Aurora so it stung more. Fact remains, the real issue is that you have a crush on your boss and he doesn't reciprocate."

"That's not it."

"What then?"

Hours spent analyzing the weekend showed a clear pattern in Richard's behavior. Whenever we got closer or personal, Richard had a Dr. Jekyll/Mr. Hyde change of personality. Face changing from open and warm to that tough mask he always wears. The boss works hard at keeping his distance... Aurora Vanderbilt being the ultimate space-keeper.

"I'm almost sure Richard reciprocates on some level..." I tell Nikki about the dinner, our day in LA, and the way he danced with me. "But he's doing everything he can to fight his feelings."

"Why?"

"Because he's scared it could get serious."

"He's your boss. It's natural he'd have reservations."

"That's not it. Richard's scared of commitment after his incident at the altar."

"And you want a guy like that... why, exactly?"

"Look at it this way: Gerard ticked off all the right boyfriend boxes, and he was a disaster. A perfect match on paper, a cheating scum in real life. Richard may seem like the wrong guy for so many reasons, but he's not for the most important one."

"Which is?"

"The way my pulse quickens whenever I'm next to him, or the drop in my stomach I get just thinking about him."

"So you have a crush, it won't last forever. The beating heart, the stomach dives... they all disappear, eventually. You'll get used to him and get over it."

I look away, afraid to meet Nikki's eye.

"What is it?" she asks.

"This is more than a silly crush."

"What? You're in love with him now?"

I shake my head. "In love is too much. But it's something more than a crush."

"But you've never even kissed him."

I stare my roommate down. "Have you ever kissed Paul?"

Nikki blushes. "Fair enough. So, what are you going to do?"

"If Richard wants to play games, I'll play right along with him."

Fourteen

Never Play Games

On Monday morning, I kick off a new game called the shoe game. Richard likes heels, so I'm going to give him a run for his money. Even if buying new shoes is financially verboten, I've hoarded for years, and Carrie Bradshaw's closet has nothing on mine.

First, I shed the athleisure once and for all. If I can't walk to Brooklyn in stiletto heels and a pencil skirt, I can surely change before getting to the office. As for grooming, I do my makeup with the same chirurgical care I used to adopt at Évoque and pin my hair in a bun with a stick. The bun is only temporary; at the right moment, the stick will come out and the hair will cascade over my shoulders in voluminous waves.

Shoes. I go with nude patent leather pumps with a cute bow to accentuate the peep toe.

Clothes. A military green halter-top over a taupe satin maxi skirt with a vertiginous slit.

I carefully fold the top and skirt, place them in a garment bag, and fit them in my ever-present duffel bag that now has been compartmentalized. One side for me and one for Chevron. I pull on an old pair of black sweatpants, a matching sweatshirt, and my running shoes.

"Are you experiencing multiple personalities?" Nikki asks as I join her in the kitchenette.

I catch a glimpse of myself in the hall mirror and smirk. From the neck up, I'm Upper East Side, from the neck down, I'm sick-day-at-home.

"I'll change at the office. Did you make coffee?"

She nods.

I pour some into a thermos, kiss Nikki goodbye, and leave for my morning walking commute with Chevron.

When I get to the office, no one's there so I use the restroom to get changed. Besides the need for privacy, the early hour will help with the ridiculous amount of work I have to do: write two or three pieces on Saturday night, buy and match pictures to each article, investigate Maison Vanderbilt, and maintain all my other regular features. *Whoa.*

An hour later, it takes two steps through the door before Indira wolf whistles at me and asks, "Where are you going dressed up like that?"

"Flash news: I dress posh. Love me or love me." I'm tired of all this hipster, grunge, athleisure nonsense.

Indira drops in her chair and spins toward me smiling. "Hell, girl. Love the attitude. How was LA?"

I give her an upbeat version, leaving out Richard's escapades and our argument, and focusing on my dance with Christian Slade instead.

When Richard arrives, I oh-so-casually send a document to the printer and get up, removing the pin from my hair. The path from my desk to the print station and the one from the entrance door to Richard's office are on two parallel lines in opposite directions. The boss hasn't spotted me yet as he's reading a text. When he finally looks up and we lock eyes, I silently count... one... two...

On three, Richard's gaze flicks down to my shoes.

A second before we meet in the middle I say, "Morning, boss."

Let's pretend nothing ever happened.

Richard's eyes—somewhat wide—snap back to my face.

"Morning." The boss gives me a curt nod and continues on

his way.

I get to the printer, retrieve my copy, and walk back. From behind his desk, Richard watches me like a hawk the entire time. He's not the only one. Indira scrutinizes me with the slyness of a fox.

In fact, as soon as I sit back at my desk, a chat window pops up on the computer screen.

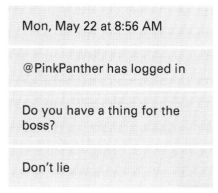

Mon, May 22 at 8:56 AM

@PinkPanther has logged in

Do you have a thing for the boss?

Don't lie

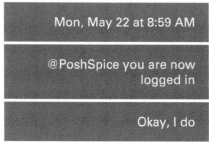

Mon, May 22 at 8:59 AM

@PoshSpice you are now logged in

Okay, I do

It's easier to tell the truth via instant messaging. Full disclosure: I didn't pick my chat nickname.

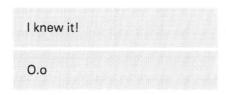

I knew it!

O.o

Something happened in LA?

Boss slept with my nemesis

And the shoes are revenge?

He seems to have a thing for footwear

Yeah, he does

At least for yours

:)

Think I'm hopeless?

If someone can straighten up the boss...

That's you, girl

Just be careful

Will do

Gotta get back to work

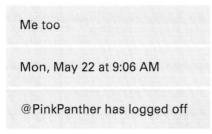

Me too

Mon, May 22 at 9:06 AM

@PinkPanther has logged off

Mon, May 22 at 9:07 AM

@PoshSpice you are now logged off

We exchange a got-your-back stare and resume our respective tasks.

I spend the rest of the morning threading interviews with pieces of gossip and shuffling professional shots of the gala. At lunch, I take my break alone to call the ex-colleague, Melanie, who had the story on Maison Vanderbilt. She's very skittish at first but then agrees to meet me tonight to tell me what she knows. After the call, I cut the break short, and my butt doesn't leave its chair for the rest of the day.

"Walker." Richard's voice startles me. "What are you still doing here?"

I lift my gaze from the screen. Outside, it's already dark, and the office is empty.

"Adding the finishing touches to my LA posts. Christian will be happy with the piece on his charity."

Richard's expression shifts oh-so-slightly from friendly to an enigmatic frown. The same one he had at Disney Hall when he took Christian's place on the dance floor.

"Sure he will," the boss comments.

"Want to see it?"

"Maybe tomorrow. Why don't you call it a night?"

I look at the time. "Oh, it doesn't matter. I have an appointment at nine-thirty."

The frown deepens. "A date?"

Richard's gaze wanders to my thighs where the slit of my skirt has opened a bit too much.

I cross my legs. "No, work. I'm meeting an ex-colleague to gather info on that Maison Vanderbilt story."

"Want company?"

"No, it's better if I talk to her alone. I don't want to spook the source. Last thing I need is to walk in on her with a stranger. She still works at Évoque, and going behind their back isn't easy."

"Is the appointment in Brooklyn?"

"No, downtown."

"Get your stuff, I'm giving you a lift home."

"Why?"

"It's dark. You shouldn't walk home alone this late."

I'm tempted to say I'm a big girl and point out that this is not the same New York of the eighties. But I'm so tired I'd gladly skip all the fuss of changing and walking home.

"Come on, Chevron," I call. "We're going home."

"*Woof.*"

I haven't attached her leash yet so that as soon as we exit the office, Chevron launches herself into the hall.

"*Ouch!*" someone screams.

There's a teenage girl sitting on the floor of our landing who's trying to fend off Chevron's overenthusiastic reception.

I dash after the pup, trying to grab her by the collar while apologizing to the girl. "I'm so sorry. I didn't expect someone to be out here. But she doesn't bite, I promise."

"It's okay," the girl says, cuddling Chevron. "She's the

cutest thing."

I manage to drag my overexcited puppy off the girl, who looks a bit too sad for her age.

"Hey, are you all right?" I ask.

The girl rolls her eyes. "Yeah, just waiting for my mom to finish work." She points at the door to her left.

I follow her finger to a plaque on the wall.

Vivian Hessington
Attorney at Law
Family Law — Divorce Attorney

The only other door on our floor opens, and a tall guy with a mop of curly dark hair comes out.

We all exchange a polite greeting and then his blue eyes widen when he spots the girl on the floor. "Tegan."

"Hi, Luke," the girl says.

The girl and the newcomer seem familiar with each other. Suddenly, I remember the shouted conversation I overheard the first day I came here. The woman was screaming for the man to keep out of her daughter's life. And the man was yelling back how someone ought to intervene since her mother didn't seem up to the task. So this Luke is Mr. Meddling. I read the plaque next to his door.

Lucas Keller
Psychologist
Marriage Counseling, Couples Therapy, Family
Specialist

Mmm, interesting pairing.

I never noticed we were sharing the floor with a divorce attorney and a couple therapist.

"What is she doing?" Luke asks, sounding mad.

"She's working late," the girl says. "Big surprise…"

"Up," Luke offers her a hand. "Come wait inside my office."

They disappear behind the door just as the elevator arrives. I attach Chevron's leash and follow the boss inside.

Richard scoffs. "What's the point of having kids and then acting like they don't exist?"

"That seems a little harsh. You don't know that girl's mother. The woman is probably doing the best she can."

"It's not the first time our neighbors have argued about the girl."

"Still not your place to judge."

Richard gives me a hard stare. "You seemed pretty quick on passing judgments yesterday."

Ah well, Richard, gut-wrenching jealousy does turn me into an ugly person.

I can't really say what I'm thinking, so I keep quiet, already regretting taking the boss up on his offer for a lift home.

***

Richard drives some sort of vintage sports car. I'm not sure what the make is, but I gather at first glance what the car isn't: cheap, ordinary, American. The wheel is on the wrong side so I have to mount from the left. Richard hops in next to me, starts the engine, and drives away at an alarming speed.

After only two turns, I'm already convinced I'm going to die. Sitting on the left side of a car in a right-driving country is no fun. It gives me the impression we'll slam into the opposing traffic at any second. I turn to Richard to protest but find I can't.

The boss is looking straight ahead with a fierce, assured expression. One hand on the wheel, the other on the gear stick. His feet work the pedals, and our speed increases once again.

Then it hits me. That's how James Bond gets all his women. It's the sporty British car. Or the speed. The adrenaline? *Oh, who am I kidding! It's the pilot—and his stupidly sexy forearms!*

"Enjoying the ride?" said pilot asks.

"More wondering if I'm going to make it home in one piece." I sulk. "You always drive like this?"

"I can slow down if it bothers you."

Please don't. "Yeah, thank you."

"*Oooooooooooooooooowhoo,*" Chevron howls her remonstrations at the reduction in speed.

Richard laughs. "At least one of my girls knows how driving should be done."

His girls? How am I one of his girls? Does he mean one of the girls in *his* car?

I spend the rest of the ride overanalyzing Richard's choice of possessive pronoun and don't even realize when he pulls onto my street.

"Sure you don't want company?" Richard asks.

"No, thanks. As I said, my source is skittish."

"Look at you, already protecting your sources. Next thing I know, you'll go for a Pulitzer."

I roll my eyes and exit the car, whistling for Chevron to follow me. When she jumps off, I secure her leash and lean my head back inside. "Thank you for the ride." Richard is struggling to look me in the eye, and in the eye only, given how deep the neckline of my top is in this position. "See you in the morning."

"Morning. Good night, I mean," he says, choked.

With a smile, I close the door. Richard waits for me to get inside before he burns rubber.

I barely have time to let Chevron in, say, "Hi," to Nikki, and dash out again. I ignore my self-imposed austerity regime and take a cab uptown. The nude heels are too high to walk comfortably in, and I'm too lazy to take the subway.

My phone pings halfway through the ride. It's a series of messages from Melanie, the ex-colleague who supposedly had the dirt on the Vanderbilts. I hope the office gossip is reliable. If after all my boasting to Richard I show up empty-handed, I'll die of shame. And I can't stand the thought of Aurora beating me once again, even if she isn't aware that we've engaged in a new fight.

> I won't be there tonight

> The person you need to talk to is waiting at table 18

> Please do not contact me again

I almost expect to receive a follow-up, "your phone will self-destruct in ten seconds" message, but that's it. Good thing I didn't accept Richard's offer to come along. I don't even know who I'm meeting.

The bar Melanie—or this other person—picked is not very spy movie. The vibe is more standard Manhattan post-work drink: low lights, lounge music, expensive cocktails. I follow the table numbering to eighteen where a woman in her middle/late thirties is sitting, a dry martini in front of her. Brown hair, blue eyes, dark suit—I lower my gaze—*cool shoes*. We'll get along just fine.

"Hello." I stop next to the table. "I'm Blair Walker, Melanie's friend."

"Oh, hi." The woman gets up to shake my hand. "I'm Alison."

I sit opposite her and order a diet Coke, wanting to keep a clear head. To break the ice, we do a small round of get-to-know-you chitchat until she seems relaxed enough, and I move on to the real reason for this meeting.

"So, Maison Vanderbilt. Mind if I take notes?" I ask, fishing in my bag for a notepad and a pen. How old-fashioned of me. I almost went and bought a tape recorder but it seemed a bit much, and I wasn't sure a bar with music would've been the best place to use one.

"Please, go ahead," Alison says.

"Okay, ready to get started?"

She nods and takes a sip of her cocktail.

"First, I need to know if you'd rather have your name on the record or if you want to remain an anonymous source."

"Anonymous."

"Good." *It's not good.* Anonymous sources pose an issue of credibility, and Richard is already all over me with this investigation. I hope at least Alison has some definitive proof. "So, Melanie didn't tell me much over the phone. She only said you're the one who came to her with a potential story two years ago and that she'd arrange this meeting."

"Yeah, Melanie and I were roommates in college and I knew she worked at a magazine. Even if Mel wasn't a reporter or anything, I thought she could be interested in a fashion house scandal or at least pass the info on to a real journalist." Alison keeps fidgeting with the stem of her glass. "But she didn't. She told me her Editor-in-Chief had killed the story and forbidden her to pass it on. I was surprised when she called me. I was sure no one at Northwestern would touch the info with a ten-foot pole."

"Oh, I'm not with Northwestern. Not anymore."

Alison lets out a nervous laugh. "That explains the call then.

Where do you work?"

"At an online-only outlet. Here, let me show you." I use my tablet to show her the homepage.

"And how come you're interested in this story?"

"If the Vanderbilts are committing tax fraud the public has… a right to know."

Alison gives me a long, piercing stare. "Care to share the real reason now?"

If I want her to trust me, I should return the courtesy.

I sigh. "Rebecca and Aurora Vanderbilt cost me my job."

"How?"

"I was in a race for a promotion with Aurora and her mother thwarted me with money. It got Aurora promoted, and yours truly fired."

Alison nods and leans back in her chair. "That makes two of us."

"You were fired?"

She nods.

"So what was your relationship with Maison Vanderbilt?"

"I used to work there as an accountant."

"Can we cite our source as a former company accountant?"

"Yes." *Oh, finally a welcome surprise.* "Just don't specify male or female and how much time I worked there."

"Just for my personal record, how long was that?"

"Nine years."

"Then what happened?"

"I asked the wrong question and three months later I got the ax."

"And you're sure the two are related."

"Positive."

"Were you the only employee let go?"

"Oh, no. They're not that stupid. HR called it a functional restructuring and fired eight other people alongside me, all accountants. Perfect cover up, really. That way I couldn't sue them for wrongful termination."

"Which is also why you're allowing us to disclose that you were an accountant there. With nine people fired at the same time, they can't point the finger at anyone in particular."

"Exactly. I'm using their smarts against them."

"Great, so tell me what happened. Start at the beginning and don't leave out anything, however small the detail may seem to you."

"It all started when I noticed repeated monthly payments going to an off-shore company that didn't seem to provide Maison Vanderbilt with any real service..."

I lean back in my chair and listen to Alison's tale.

Fifteen

Never Dwell on the Past

"So you've no *actual* proof," Richard says, after listening to my account of the chat with Alison—whose name and gender I've kept private.

For the past half hour, I've been watching his frown get deeper. We're facing each other on opposite sides of his desk, and the outright enthusiasm I felt this morning is bleeding out, stabbed in the chest by every new crease that appears on Richard's forehead.

"Define *actual* proof," I say. "I have an ex-accountant on record—"

"You have an anonymous source."

"So what? We can say they were an accountant at Maison Vanderbilt and they're sure the company had a false billing scheme in place."

Richard rolls up his sleeves. "Had or *has?*"

Oh, no. I won't be distracted by his forearms today. *Eye on the prize, Blair.* "My source can only testify to what was going on while under… their employment." This conversation is draining. How long until I accidentally slip and mention Alison's gender?

"Meaning the scheme might not be in place anymore. Or that it could be under completely different names and shell companies."

"It doesn't matter. The scheme did exist and we have everything we need to expose Maison Vanderbilt."

"Except hard evidence."

"We don't need hard evidence. The IRS can get them after

142

we tip them off with the exposé, and once the tax police start looking, they'll find something. Because the fraud *did* happen."

"So says you."

"So says their ex-accountant."

"Oh, please. Your source is just some sour ex-employee who was fired and who has a big, fat chip on their shoulder. Same as you."

That last comment strikes where it hurts. Nostrils flaring, I say, "Chip or not, the facts remain. Neither of us is lying."

"I can't publish a story based on hearsay."

I clench my fists and try not to grind my teeth. "So you're pulling the plug?"

Richard massages his temples. "Not yet. We're going to get a second opinion."

***

Two days later, we head to the-middle-of-nowhere, upstate New York, to meet with an "expert" financial reporter.

The drive is no less an aphrodisiac than the other night, only this time much longer. My hormones are all over the place. Chevron is going crazy in the backseat, too, only she's crazy happy, not randy. My dog enjoys her speed and luxury cars.

Richard's contact, Michael, welcomes us at the gates of his house—a mansion in the middle of a forest.

Very scenic, only mildly unpractical.

Our host is in his late forties, but fit for his age, with salt-and-pepper hair, and intelligent blue eyes. After Richard parks the car and lets Chevron loose in the fenced backyard, Michael shows us inside to his study.

The walls are lined with bookshelves, and everything—desk, shelves, chairs—is in dark walnut. The floor is covered in rugs, and there's a big, oval table in the center of the room. *Very*

English country quarters.

Michael's wife appears five minutes later with tea and cookies. "Hi, I'm Susan," she greets us, dropping the tray on the table.

"Blair. Nice to meet you."

"Richard."

"Oh, the pleasure is all mine. I just wanted to bring you some treats before the meeting started."

"Thank you," Richard and I both say.

"The cookies are homemade," Susan explains, "dairy-free, and the eggs come straight from our hens, so don't worry, they're happy chickens."

Where do I sign to have Michael and Susan adopt me?

Next to me, Richard almost chokes on a bite of cookie. I smile and give the boss a stare that says, "See, everyone is concerned with chicken welfare."

Susan leaves and Michael turns to us. "Richard, why don't you tell me what this story we couldn't discuss over the phone is? I'm intrigued."

Richard doesn't reply.

I raise my gaze from the table and catch them both looking at me. Oh, the boss expects *me* to do the talking. And here I was, too busy deciding how many cookies I could eat without appearing like a total pig.

"So." I swallow the last bit of crunchy deliciousness and give Michael the same report I gave Richard two days ago.

The journalist listens patiently and doesn't interrupt once so that when I'm done talking, I have to ask for his opinion. "What's your take?"

Michael strokes the back of his head. "Your story does add up, but you don't have definitive proof."

Richard speaks before I can. "Would you run an article based only on what you've heard today?"

"I would"—Michael gives him a piercing stare—"if my editor backed me."

I love you, Michael!

Richard frowns. "And would any *sane* editor back you?"

"You have a source and a credible one. I'd say it'd be fifty-fifty…"

Michael's implied meaning is all too clear. *Depending on the attributes of said editor.*

Richard shakes his head.

"Whatever you do," Michael continues, "you need to ask Maison Vanderbilt for a statement. They can refuse, and you put in your piece they weren't available for comment. But you're required to contact a representative beforehand and give them the chance to refute your case."

A mean idea is taking form in my head. "What if we asked Rebecca Vanderbilt point-blank?"

Richard shakes his head. "She'd just deny it."

"What if she couldn't?" I insist.

"You want to base your strategy on the hope that Rebecca Vanderbilt doesn't lie?" Richard snaps. "Think again."

"That's not what I meant. We'd have to trap her with our line of questioning."

Richard crosses his arms. "Give me an example."

"We ask her if she's ever heard of Heron LLC. If she lies and says no, then we ask how come Maison Vanderbilt paid millions in management fees to that very company for at least three consecutive fiscal years."

"All that would achieve is perhaps for you to make Rebecca Vanderbilt blush, at best." Richard isn't budging. "No one would see her reaction, and she'd then work to cover her tracks even more thoroughly. If she hasn't already."

I expected this argument. "What if everyone *did* see it?"

"And how would you make that happen?"

"We could tape her."

"Walker," Richard scoffs. "This isn't a spy movie. You can't go around taping people. She'd sue the second the video aired."

"What if she'd given us permission to tape her?"

"And why would she do that?"

"I know this might sound far-fetched, but hear me out." I push both of my hands forward, palms up, to prevent objections. "What if we contacted her saying Inceptor Magazine wants to do an interview? Something about how Rebecca Vanderbilt built her fashion empire. Or how good Maison Vanderbilt is to the community with all the charities it supports. Or how Rebecca is a role model for so many young women. Then mid-interview, *bam!*" I slam my hand on the table. "We drop the bomb and ask her all the questions we want about tax evasion."

Richard doesn't reject the idea outright, and Michael is staring at me with an appreciative "holy s—, girl" expression, so I press on. "At that point, the cameras would be rolling and Rebecca couldn't possibly refuse to answer or she might as well admit she's guilty. All we have to do is come up with the right questions…"

"I can help with that," Michael offers.

I turn to him. "Thank you." Then back to Richard. "And even if she left in a rage at some point, we would have everything on the record."

"What makes you think Rebecca Vanderbilt would even agree to an interview with you? You're not exactly friendly with her daughter."

I blush, and then punch below the belt. "But you are."

"Not that much," Richard says, and my heart leaps. At least their little gathering in LA was a bona fide one-night stand.

"Anyway," Richard continues, "even if I were close to her, what would you have me do? Trick Aurora into ruining her mother's life?"

"Would you do it?"

A girl can hope.

"It's out of the question."

And have her hopes crushed. Anyway, I wouldn't have respected Richard if he'd said yes.

"And what if I got the interview all by myself?" I ask.

"If you can do it without dropping my name."

"I'll have to use the magazine name, and you're the Editor-in-Chief."

"As long as you leave me out of it personally, it'd be fine."

"Perfect! Are you giving me the green light to try?"

"Not yet." Richard drums his fingers on the table. "What if Rebecca Vanderbilt were to sue?"

"For what? We'd make her sign a disclaimer beforehand granting us permission to air the interview."

"What if she sues for slander?"

"They can win a lawsuit for slander only if the accusation is false," Michael says. "And if they do sue you, it'd give you the right to access their books to prove your innocence. I doubt any lawyer in his right mind would initiate that kind of lawsuit with a guilty client."

"So we don't risk anything?" Richard asks.

"The way I see it," Michael scratches his chin. "Worst-case scenario, the interview is a YouTube flop and you've made an enemy for life. Best-case scenario, it goes viral, and the IRS picks up the investigation where you left off."

"You think that could really happen?" I ask.

Michael nods. "Half the government's investigations start from anonymous or public tips."

"Then why don't we just tip off the IRS and let them do all the work?" Richard asks.

"Ah." Michael sighs. "In that case, there's no guarantee they'd follow up on the tip, but if you make a big public splash…"

Richard sighs. "I really have no choice here, do I?"

"Sorry, buddy," Michael shrugs. "The girl has you cornered."

Michael winks at me and I beam back. I can hardly sit in my chair.

"So the interview is a go?" I ask.

Richard looks at me and gives a resigned nod.

***

A week later, my phone starts vibrating on my desk. The caller ID—recently changed—shows, Billy Loomis. Okay, my ex-boyfriend isn't exactly a serial killer, and he didn't try to murder me and all my friends while wearing a stupid white mask. But still, I couldn't keep Gerard as Edward Cullen.

I let the call go unanswered. Two minutes later the phone rings again, and again a third time. At the fourth call, I press ignore, letting Gerard know I'm willfully ignoring his calls. The phone goes silent after that.

Yay, he's given up.

A mail banner flashes on the screen.

Nope.

I HAVE NEVER

Date: Thu, June 1 at 10:22 AM
From: gerard.wakefield@aol.com
To: blair.walker@yahoo.com
Subject: I'm sorry, please don't ruin my life

Blair, please. I know you're mad at me and that I behaved like a total bastard with you. There are no excuses for what I did and I'm so very sorry I threatened to sue you and for everything else. But I got scared and didn't know what else to do. You can't talk to the partners at my firm. It would destroy me. Annihilate me. Please, I'm willing to negotiate a settlement with your lawyer. Whatever you want, you can have. But please not a word to anyone at my firm. If you can find even the smallest shred of compassion in you, please try to forgive me.

Sincerely,
Gerard

Wow, talk about a groveling apology! I know Gerard doesn't really regret what he did and that he's just scared I'll use the affair against him. Still, a crappy apology is better than no apology. I had completely forgotten about my threats to expose him. Does he really think I'd do something so mean and spiteful? *Yes, probably because he's the kind of person who would.* I realize then that I never really knew Gerard, and he must've not known me. Anyway, despite him behaving like vermin, the bastard has suffered enough. I don't want to ruin anyone's life. I quickly tap a reply.

Date: Thu, June 1 at 10:25 AM
From: blair.walker@yahoo.com
To: gerard.wakefield@aol.com
Subject: Re: I'm sorry, please don't ruin my life

Gerard, do us both a favor and relax. I was never going to sue you. I'm not that kind of person. Please stop calling me.

Blair

I'm about to press send when I change my mind. If Gerard was a shitty boyfriend, something he is not is a shitty lawyer. I press delete and type a different message.

Date: Thu, June 1 at 10:27 AM
From: blair.walker@yahoo.com
To: gerard.wakefield@aol.com
Subject: Re: I'm sorry, please don't ruin my life

I need a legal favor. Can you write a bulletproof disclaimer for an interview? Do this for me and you're off the hook.

Blair

Rebecca Vanderbilt's PA has agreed to do the interview. Even better, she insisted on having it in Maison Vanderbilt's flagship store in Manhattan. With the interview date approaching fast, I need to make sure the magazine is covered from any legal action against us. And what better advisor than my shark-lawyer ex who's willing to do about anything for me?

Gerard's reply arrives immediately.

I HAVE NEVER

Date: Thu, June 1 at 10:28 AM
From: gerard.wakefield@aol.com
To: blair.walker@yahoo.com
Subject: Re: Re: I'm sorry, please don't ruin my life

Thank you, Blair. Anything. Anything you need. Just let me know the details, and it'll be ready for you by tomorrow morning.

Thank you.
Gerard

Now we're talking.

***

I could have asked Gerard to FedEx me the finished document, but there's a part of me that wants closure. After three years of my life spent with that man, our story ended in a restaurant in less than half an hour. I need to see Gerard and be sure I'm not harboring unrequited feelings for him. The only way to know if I'm over him is if he makes me feel nothing. Total indifference is the opposite of love, not hate.

We agree to meet super early the next morning, and I make him come down to my side of Manhattan. Something he never did while we dated. I leave a moping Chevron home and go to the meeting alone.

When I get to the café, Gerard is already there sipping coffee while seated at an outside table. He hasn't spotted me yet, so I assess my reactions from the safety of my side of the street. I study him. Still good-looking, but also pompous looking—expensive suit, shoes, and tie, confident smirk, and a five-hundred-dollar haircut. In short, a handsome prick. But definitely not someone I'm in love with. My breath isn't in my throat, I have no accelerated pulse, and my stomach remains level. Well, actually, it churns a little. If I can't have total indifference, I'll settle for total revulsion.

I cross the road. "Hi."

"Blair." Gerard stands up.

There's an awkward moment when it seems he's about to kiss me on the cheek, but my glare must be enough to dissuade him.

"Would you like a coffee?" he asks.

"No, thanks. I'd like to get this over with as quickly as possible."

"Sure." He reaches down into a briefcase and hands me a folder. "Here's everything you need. Get Rebecca Vanderbilt's signature on the dotted line and you're covered. Can I ask what this is about?"

"No," I reply sharply. "You'll find out by the end of next week, anyway." I tap the folder. "Is this the real deal? Bulletproof like I asked?"

"Blair, you make Rebecca Vanderbilt sign that document and you're not wearing a bulletproof jacket"—he knocks on the wooden table—"you're standing in a nuclear bunker."

"Great. I guess I owe you a thank you."

Gerard smiles in a way I used to find endearing, but now only seems sleazy.

"Not at all," he says, then takes another folder out of the briefcase. "If you could just sign this, we're done."

I eye the folder suspiciously. "What's that?"

"The confidentiality agreement I sent you," Gerard replies, nonplussed.

"I'm not signing a confidentiality agreement."

He turns red from neck to ears. "Was this a trap? Your petty way to get revenge? You make me work for you and then you ruin me?"

"No, I'm not evil. Just because I'm not signing a piece of paper, it doesn't mean I'll go tell on you and Laura the second I leave here. Don't worry, it was never my intention."

"Why won't you sign the confidentiality agreement, then?"

"Gerard, forget it. You'll have to take me at my word." I get up. "But you can relax, as, contrary to you, I *am* trustworthy." I swing my bag over my shoulder and without waiting for a reply, I wave and say, "Have a nice life."

Always wanted to say that to somebody.

***

That same morning I go over the details of the interview with Richard.

"The equipment, plus video and audio technicians, are booked," I say. "The date is set, and here's the disclaimer for Rebecca Vanderbilt to sign." I hand Richard the document Gerard drafted. "It should be ironclad."

Richard skim-reads the pages. "Wonderful." His eyes pause on the legal stamp at the end of the document. "How were you able to afford Goldstein, Smidch, and Vander? They're a very expensive firm."

I shrug. "My ex works there."

A shadow crosses Richard's face. "You're still in contact with him?"

"No, not really. Let's just say he owed me a favor."

"He did this for you after you threw a plate of spaghetti over his head?"

"Gerard deserved the spaghetti, and he knows it."

"But why would you even ask him after everything he did?"

"What's the big deal?" *Why is Richard getting so worked up?*

"We needed legal advice, and Gerard is a kickass lawyer. Plus, I wanted to see him again to see how it'd make me feel."

Richard purses his lips. Seems like he's dying to ask what my findings were, but knows he can't without being inappropriate. *Aha!* The boss *is* British after all.

"So, when's the interview?" Richard asks instead.

"Monday."

"And you plan to make it go live on…?"

"The following Friday. I don't want to give Rebecca Vanderbilt time to pull tricks out of her sleeve. No matter if we have the best disclaimer ever written."

Richard sighs. "Then by next weekend, we'll know if we still have a magazine or not."

"About that. I wanted you to know how much I appreciate the trust you're placing in me. I know this interview is causing you more than a headache and a few sleepless nights. And I can't say enough how thankful I am you're letting me run the story anyway. Even if it means facing a potential lawsuit…"

"Hey." Richard finally cracks a smile. "We wouldn't be a serious newspaper if we didn't get a lawsuit every now and then. Walker, you have my complete trust."

"Thank you, boss. I won't let you down."

Sixteen

Never Pick a Fight

Monday morning, at eight sharp, I'm shaking hands with the very woman I'm about to ruin. I've rehearsed every question several times with both Richard and Michael. Our financial expert has also agreed to write a complementary article to go with the interview. After a weekend spent obsessing over every little detail that could go wrong, I'm ready.

When the introductions are over, I inhale deeply and hand Rebecca Vanderbilt the disclaimer.

"If you could sign here, we can get started right away."

"What's this?" she snaps.

"Oh, only a disclaimer that allows us to air the interview. It's standard procedure."

I hold my breath as she scans the fine print. If she doesn't sign this, I'm toast. I can't ask her any of the burning questions.

Rebecca hands the document to her PA. "What do you think?"

The woman turns the pages with hawk-like eyes, and for the first time, I'm worried. Miss PA doesn't look like a fool.

"Seems pretty standard, but I don't think you should sign any document without a lawyer checking it first." Then she stares up at me. "We can have our in-house attorney go over the disclaimer and send it back signed after the interview."

Sweat pools under my armpits and on my upper lip. "I'm sorry, but that won't be possible. Without your explicit permission, we can't so much as record Mrs. Vanderbilt saying hello, let alone record footage of the inside of the store. If she doesn't sign, we can't proceed with the interview at all." The sweating worsens. I try to inconspicuously wipe away the cold droplets on my forehead.

The mean PA woman doesn't buy my stream of BS. "Then I suggest we postpone until our lawyers have had time to review these papers."

"Nonsense," Rebecca interjects. "Give me the document."

"Mrs. Vanderbilt," the PA insists. "I strongly suggest you reconsider."

Luckily, Aurora's mother is not very good at taking advice.

With a wave of her hand, she says, "Oh, please. I wouldn't be where I am today if I hadn't taken a risk or two down the road. Pen!"

The reluctant PA hands her a Montblanc and Rebecca happily signs her own death warrant. *Gotcha!*

After three makeup retouches, The Madame is finally ready to go on screen. We sit on the apricot couches outside the fitting rooms, wait a few seconds for the lighting technician to adjust the lamps, and then we're rolling…

After a few introductory questions, I start laying my trap. "Mrs. Vanderbilt, I don't know if you remember, but the last time I saw you, we were in LA at Christian's Slade charity ball for his Teachers without Postcodes fair education project. Given how busy you are as CEO of Maison Vanderbilt, do you often find time to attend charitable events like that one?"

"Coming from a family of entrepreneurs and being an entrepreneur myself, one of the key aspects of my work ethic is giving back to the community. That's why I always make time for public service, no matter how busy my schedule is. At Maison Vanderbilt, we constantly strain to give more than our due, contributing to various charities on top of our legal obligations."

"As it happens, Maison Vanderbilt is one of the most

generous companies when it comes to charity." I shuffle my papers to check the numbers. "My records show that last year alone, you contributed over five million dollars to different projects. With a specific focus on youth and education."

"Yes, exactly. We focus in particular on nurturing the next generation of talent. It's extremely important to foster tomorrow's leaders as they represent our future."

"Public education in our country is mainly funded through taxes—property taxes for the most part, but also state and federal taxes. So what do you think of companies that use tax havens to hide assets and pay fewer taxes than what they really owe?"

"Well, they're obviously cheating society and robbing communities blind. Everyone has to do their part."

"Those are sage words, Mrs. Vanderbilt, and it's interesting hearing them coming from you. What about yourself? Have you ever had any connection to an offshore company?"

"Maison Vanderbilt has many international branches." Rebecca grimaces. "Some of them are located in countries with taxation incentives. It's common practice for multinational companies to-to… anyway, I don't see what the point of this question is… It feels almost as if you were accusing me of something."

"Are you at all familiar with a company called Heron LLC?"

She pales. "No, why should I?"

"So you've never heard the name Heron LLC. It's a company based in the Cayman Islands, a notorious tax haven."

"Never," she says haughtily, moving her chin up. "Can we return to the original scope of this interview? Why are we talking about the Cayman Islands? Unless of course it's to discuss our newest resort collection." Rebecca lets out a high-pitched laugh.

"In a moment." *Oh, you're not wiggling out of this one.* "But you see, I find it weird the name Heron LLC is unfamiliar to you. According to a former employee of Maison Vanderbilt, your company used to pay millions in management fees to Heron every year."

"This is nonsense." Rebecca searches with her eyes for help, looking very much like a trapped animal. No one comes to her aid.

Luck is on my side as her PA seems to have vanished after she made sure the interview was going smoothly, leaving her boss completely at my mercy.

"Mrs. Vanderbilt, isn't paying management fees to an offshore company one of the easiest means of tax evasion?"

"I don't know what you're talking about."

"Just to be clear, as CEO of Maison Vanderbilt, you're denying ever committing tax fraud."

"You've no proof of these absurd allegations you're making."

"I have the word of a former accountant at your company. Anyway, are you claiming I've no proof or that the fact never subsisted?"

Now she stands up. "This interview is over. *Over!* You silly girl. Dare make public a second of this reckless ambush and you'll never be able to show your face in Manhattan ever again. I'll make sure no one ever hires you."

I stand up as well. "I already have a job, thank you."

"Not when I sue your little magazine for every cent it has."

"I'm sure any judge will recognize the truth of our statements, or the IRS will. Mrs. Vanderbilt, I'm afraid it will be you hiding your face around Manhattan when this interview goes live. Because rest assured, it *will* go live…"

That's when a composed, supposedly classy, if not very honest woman completely loses it and turns into a bratty child. Screaming and destroying everything in her path.

***

A few days later, everyone in the office has gathered behind my desk to watch the video of the interview on my computer. Well, everyone except for Richard, who, for some reason, has not shown up to work yet. I hate the disappointment I feel at him not being here to witness my success.

Where the hell is the boss?

"Uuuuuhh-uuuuh," my colleagues cheer as they watch Rebecca Vanderbilt hit the camera.

I've uploaded the final footage to YouTube this morning and Hugo, our News Editor, has posted Michael's supplementary article on our homepage.

"This is my favorite part," Hugo says. "When she grabs the camera and sends it crashing down."

"No, no," Indira says. "You have to wait until the very end."

We all keep our eyes glued to the screen. Now we can only see the marble floor of the Maison Vanderbilt flagship store through the cracked camera glass. And, of course, hear Rebecca Vanderbilt's threats to sue us. She screamed a lot, and we had to add several censoring "beeps" to the audio file.

"Wait for it," Indira mutters, "wait for it… There it goes."

Rebecca Vanderbilt stomps her expensive stiletto on the camera and the video goes black.

Indira clicks her tongue. "Best finale ever."

"Yeah, pretty cool!" Hugo agrees.

"I'm posting a screenshot of the stiletto of death on Instagram," Saffron says.

"Refresh the page," Ada asks.

I do as she says.

"How many views?"

"Fifty thousand," I say.

"How long ago did you upload this?" Hugo asks.

I check the clock window on the screen. "About an hour. Are fifty thousand views any good?"

"Are you kidding me?" Saffron asks. "You're on the road to get batshit crazy viral, girl."

I smile. "I hope everyone sees this, and that the IRS indicts them."

Zane's landline rings, and he walks back to his desk to answer. As soon as he picks up the receiver, he signals for us to quiet down. We do, while also taking the opportunity to eavesdrop on the conversation. Zane is in charge of distribution and it sounds like he's negotiating with some other news outlet who wants to air the interview. And I don't want to be too optimistic, but it seems like he's talking to a TV network.

TV or not, I don't finish listening in on the conversation because, at that moment, Richard walks through the front doors. Too happy to see him, I get up and almost run toward him. I catch myself just in time and stop a few feet away. Was I really about to launch myself at him and throw my arms around his neck?

"Hi," I say. "Where were you? The interview went live an hour ago!"

Richard gives me an awkward smile. "I hit a bit of a road bump."

"Oh, what happened?"

"I had to see Aurora."

Ice spreads through my veins. "Vanderbilt?"

"The one and only."

"Why?"

Richard sighs. "I wanted to give her fair warning. I didn't want her to go to work today and get blindsided by the story breaking." He shrugs. "I owed her that much."

"I'm sure her mother must've told her by now," I say a bit too aggressively.

"No, apparently she hadn't. And anyway, nobody knew we were going live today, so..."

That's very decent of him. I still wish he hadn't done it. The thought of him and Aurora together, no matter the circumstances, makes me see red.

"How did she take it?"

"At first she wouldn't believe me. I don't think she was involved in the fraud. Her mother must've kept all their shady dealings from her."

"And after you explained, did she believe you?"

"Oh, no." Richard shakes his head. "Once the shock was over, she got mental! She tried to convince me not to publish the interview and once I refused, she... ah... threw her coffee at me."

I cover my mouth with one hand. "Did you get burned?"

"No, it was iced. But I still had to go home and change."

Right, his curls still seem a bit damp. Mmm, I have to fight hard with my limbs not to run a hand up the back of his neck.

"Anyway." Richard moves toward the group assembled at my desk. "How are the first responses?"

Ada clicks the mouse. "Sixty thousand views already."

"Social media is going crazy," Saffron says.

"CNN wants to run the story on *CNN Today!*" Zane puffs his chest out.

"CNN," I screech. "Are you kidding me?"

"I kid you not!" He smiles.

Richard pats my shoulder. "Well done!"

161

I beam at him, trying not to melt under his touch.

"Now," the boss adds in a more practical tone. "Can we manage the extra traffic to our website?" he asks, looking at the techies.

"I'll make sure we get some extra server capacity," one says.

The entire tech team scurries back to their computers.

"All right," Richard says, addressing the whole office. "Let's make sure we run a tight ship today and then we can all go out to celebrate tonight!"

Everyone shouts their approval and even Chevron contributes to the general enthusiasm with a loud howl.

***

By the end of the day, I have a better understanding of what "going viral" means. The hashtag #MaisonVanderFraud is trending on Twitter, we've reached over a million views on YouTube, and the story is all over the media. Both traditional and social.

At six thirty, Richard walks to the center of the open space and claps his hands to get everyone's attention.

"All right, people." The office quiets down. "This week has been incredible, and today has been an unprecedented success. It couldn't have happened without your combined effort. Blair, thank you for bringing in the story and pulling off a magnificent piece of investigative journalism. Zane, thanks for handling the TV rights." Each announcement is followed by thunderous applause. "Saffron, for fueling the Social Media craze. Our techies, for making sure our website didn't crash. Everyone else, for your support." Richard lets the applause die before speaking again. "Now it's Friday night, and I don't know about you, but I can't wait for the weekend to get started. So what do you say we all go out for a drink to celebrate?"

Richard's proposal is approved by a standing ovation.

He lingers by my desk. "Walker, are you coming?"

"I'm not sure." The boss seems disappointed, so I add, "It's just that I don't know if a bar is a good place for Chevron."

"Right, I hadn't thought of that. What if I take Chevron to my house and join you guys later?"

"Are you sure it's not a problem?" I ask.

He kneels down to pet her with both hands, and I swear I've never seen a dog so ecstatic. "Nah, I'm sure this beauty won't wreck the place, and anyway, I can give you a lift home afterward. You can't walk home alone in the middle of the night."

"Okay." I surrender the leash and the duffel bag.

As we queue in front of the elevators, Indira leans in and whispers in my ear, "Smooth."

I scowl at her without replying.

Outside the building, I pat Chevron goodbye and say to Richard, "See you at the bar."

As I watch the two of them go, a million scenarios start playing in my head at once. Richard kissing me goodnight in his damned sexy car, or even better, him inviting me in before he takes me home...

My happy stream of fantasies is interrupted by my phone ringing, screen flashing with the ominous caller ID, Dolores Umbridge.

I sigh and pick up. "Hello, Mom."

The others are still waiting, so I gesture for them to keep going and that I'll meet them at the bar.

"Blair." My mother's voice rattles out of the phone's speakers. Already, from the single pronunciation tone of my name, I understand that she isn't happy with me. "What is this I've heard about you being on your tube? Is it proper for a future mother? My friends at the country club say it's a website with a questionable reputation."

"Mom, it's YouTube, and I did an interview. There's nothing questionable about it."

"An interview? So you got the editor position at Évoque? Why didn't you tell me? I can't wait to tell all my friends."

"No, Mom, I didn't." I stare at the sky, unsure what to say next. I've avoided talking to her since, well, since I was fired. My fuse for my mother has become shorter than ever and I don't care whether she approves or disapproves how I live my life anymore. So I rat myself out. "Actually, Évoque fired me."

"Fired? You? And what do you do for money?"

"I work at a different magazine."

"Which one? Is it better than Évoque?"

I think for a second. "Yeah, ten thousand times better."

"Well, what's it called?"

"Inceptor Magazine."

"I've never heard of it."

"Because it's a new online publication."

"Online? Have you gone mad? What's the publishing house, is it still Northwestern?"

"No. There's no publishing house, it's just the magazine."

"But... but... I mean, what does Gerard think about it?"

"I don't know, and I don't care. We broke up."

"Oh. Oh, goodness. What did you do?"

"*I* did nothing." *Somebody help, please.* I'm about to lose my temper big time. "*He* cheated on me."

"Ah, well, a man like him with an important job... I'm sure you can work through this crisis..."

The fuse reaches the end and I explode. "Mom, are you even listening to me? Gerard was having an affair with his secretary. There's nothing left to work on."

"So what? You'd rather be single? At your age?"

"Yeah, definitely. Single is not a dirty word, and it's better to be alone than to stay in a relationship because it looks better from the outside. I'm not you!"

Without waiting for a reply, I hang up on the momster and turn my phone off.

Arrrgh, that woman!

She still has the power to drive me crazy. Well, at least after our cozy chat she won't call me for another couple of months. Fine by me. I'm ready for a drink and to forget all about parental harassment.

Seventeen

Never Have I Ever

The atmosphere inside the bar has the peculiar cheerfulness only Friday nights can bring along. The guys are outside, seated at a large table in the prettiest back patio ever. Enclosed between brick buildings, covered in green ivy, and with string lights dangling side-to-side, it's modern and quaint at the same time.

Indira waves me over and points at the chair next to her. When I sit down she says, "I've ordered you a margarita and some veggie tacos." She pushes a glass and a plate my way.

"Thanks." I smile and take my reserved spot. "Mmm, these are delicious." I devour a full taco before touching any alcohol. "I'm ordering another round."

As I turn to attract the attention of a server, I catch Richard's eye instead. He's standing on the threshold of the garden, looking at me. Actually, seems like he's been standing there a while. Was he watching me the whole time? The hair on my nape immediately stands up. As he smiles and starts walking toward us, goose bumps rise all over my arms.

Richard sits at the head of the table, one seat away from me. "What did I miss?"

Indira replies, "Tacos and tequila."

The server who I tried to call before arrives to take the table's final orders. I ask for a salad and some other vegetarian tacos. Richard gets a beer and tacos as do most of the others.

The few nights out with my old colleagues from Évoque don't compare. Not with their calorie-counting remarks, bitchy competitiveness, and overpriced cocktails. Here, everyone's mood is relaxed and cheerful. Hugo is being a clown, telling

166

Tinder dates horror stories. Indira is giving everyone sass. And whenever Nico tries to start a serious political debate, we all boo him. The quietest is Saffron, who spends most of the night glued to her phone, giving the group sporadic updates on the number of likes, shares, and views the interview is getting.

When it reaches two million views on YouTube, Richard bangs a fist on the table. "Who's in for celebratory shots?" he shouts.

There's a general cheer of approval, and the boss leaves to fetch a server who reappears minutes later with three bottles of tequila and shot glasses.

I'm trying not to get completely wasted, so I grab the least full glass and drink only for the main toast. Richard also goes back to beer after one shot. Zane and Hugo are not so shy and peruse the bottle multiple times.

As the night progresses, my colleagues start to leave one by one, until there's only Saffron, Indira, and the boss left. We move to a smaller table. Richard carrying his beer and Saffron salvaging the only remaining half-full bottle of tequila along with the shot glasses.

The adrenaline of the day, the tequila, and Richard's proximity make it too hard for me to talk. I let Indira and Saffron lead the conversation. As we listen to the other two, I occasionally catch the boss giving me furtive looks, and smiling. *Is he eye-flirting?*

"Yo, guys," Saffron says after a while, stretching in her chair like a cat. "I'm calling it a night."

"Me too," Indira echoes.

They both get up and look at us as if to say, "You coming?"

Richard lifts his half-full glass. "Mind if I finish the beer before we go get Chevron?"

"No, sure." I get up to hug Saffron and Indira goodnight.

The former pulls me into a tight embrace. "The boss likes you," she whispers in my ear, and then she adds aloud, "See you Monday."

Richard nods, and we both watch Indira and Saffron slalom through the tables and disappear inside the main bar. And then we're alone.

There's a moment of awkward silence until Richard asks, "Want something else to drink?"

"No, I'm good. Thanks."

"Pity, there's half a bottle of good tequila left." He chugs the last of his beer and takes the bottle in his hands. Then he turns toward me with a mischievous grin. "Still convinced you'd lose at that drinking game?"

"Never have I ever? One-hundred percent."

Richard flashes me a challenging smile. "Want to give it a try?"

The smile I give back is equally wicked. "Game on."

"What were the rules again?"

"You say something daring you've never done, and if I have, I drink a shot and vice versa."

Richard grabs two clean shot glasses. "And how do we decide who loses?"

"Whoever drinks the most shots?"

His eyes sparkle as he fills the glasses. "Ladies first."

"Okay." I wrinkle my nose. "Never have I ever… cheated on someone."

Richard doesn't move. "Sorry to disappoint."

"Actually, that's no disappointment." I smile. "Your turn."

"I have never…"

"Say it properly. Never have I ever…"

"That's just a waste of words. I have never… thrown a bowl of spaghetti on somebody's head."

"You're using inside information. Not sure that's fair." I begrudgingly drink my shot.

The boss refills the glass. "Your turn."

I realize Richard knows more about me than I do about him. It'll take some guesswork to hit the right spots. "Never have I ever… gotten a tattoo."

He drinks. Mmm, interesting. Now I can't stop wondering where the tattoo is. I scan his chest for a moment before catching his gaze. Richard gives me a knowing stare as if he knew I was hoping to X-ray through his shirt and see the ink.

"I have never…" Richard pauses, "been arrested."

"You're not playing fair." The tequila burns my throat. This time I do the refill, keeping the shot glasses more than half empty. I've learned how to pace myself with alcohol.

"Never have I ever"—I think for a second—"had someone slap me across the face."

Richard gives me a wicked smile and lifts the glass to his lips.

"Ow. Deserved?"

"Some of them." He shrugs. "I have never… worn a jade dress."

"That's not even something daring."

Richard raises a mischievous brow. "I wouldn't call the dress you wore in LA *not* daring."

I blush and drink. "Never have I ever… attended boarding school."

"What's daring about boarding school?"

"You tell me."

With a naughty grin, he drinks. "I have never… woken up not knowing where I was."

I scowl and drink. This is too easy for him. "Never have I ever… punched someone."

The boss drinks.

"Did *they* deserve it?"

"Oh, yes. I have never…"

Richard and I both guess the next three until the tequila in my system makes me bold enough to step up the game a notch. "Never have I ever… been left at the altar."

Heart pounding, I wait for his reaction. Richard gives me a long stare and lifts the glass to his lips.

"So it's true," I say.

"Wouldn't have drunk otherwise."

"How did it happen?"

"Easily, she changed her mind mid-ceremony. My turn." Richard makes it clear that's all I'm going to get of his backstory. "I have never…"

After a few more rounds of the game, I'm about to reach the point of no return, so before I'm irredeemably drunk I surrender. "Okay, okay. You've made your point. I've become bad enough to lose at this stupid game. But if I drink another shot, we both know where it ends, and it's not pretty. We should play a different game."

Richard flashes me a molten stare, and for a second I'm left breathless. "Truth or dare?"

I don't know why, but the truth part seems scarier than the dare. So I say, "Dare."

"Don't move."

I sit rigidly in my chair as Richard bends his head towards my neck until his mouth is barely an inch from my collarbone. He inhales. There's no touching. Only the faint caress of Richard's breath on my skin. But it's enough to send a shiver down my spine.

"Nice perfume," he says, standing back up.

Mouth dry, I ask, "Truth or dare?"

"Dare."

"Show me your tattoo."

Richard undoes the top three buttons of his shirt, moving the fabric aside to expose his left collarbone where a small, black infinity symbol is tattooed on his skin. The little symbol stands out on his marble-like skin and it's made of words. I lean in to read, getting a peek of his toned chest as an extra perk. I swallow, concentrating hard on the tiny words and not his pectorals. Depending on where one starts reading the writing says, "Love the life you live," or "Live the life you love."

"Cool," I say, leaning back, although not before inhaling Richard's green forest scent.

Richard buttons up his shirt and I'm left mourning the wonderful sight of his almost bare chest.

"Truth or dare?" he asks.

"Truth."

"Are you still in love with your ex?"

"No," I say, shaking my head. "Not sure I ever was, really. Truth or dare?"

"Truth."

"What about you? Carrying a torch for someone?"

"Nope."

"Not even her?"

Richard's features harden. "I had enough time to move on." I'm about to ask more when he cuts me short. "Truth or dare?"

"Truth."

"Tell me something true you've never told anyone."

Let's see... "I don't fold my bedsheets. I just crumple them up in a ball and store them at the back of a drawer."

Richard laughs. "Guess I should've been more specific and asked for something embarrassing."

"Poor linen management is embarrassing." I smile. "Your

pick."

"Truth."

I tilt my head to the side. "Do you have a thing for my shoes?"

"Ah." He lowers his gaze to my feet and nods. "So you've noticed. Your turn."

"Truth."

"Ever thought of sleeping with your boss?"

In vino veritas and all that jazz, I tell the truth, "Yes. Truth or dare?"

"Truth."

"Why did you sleep with Aurora Vanderbilt in LA?"

"She was a safe choice."

I put a question mark on my face.

"She's the kind of person I could never fall for," Richard explains.

"And were you worried about… falling for someone else?"

Richard ignores the question. "Isn't it my turn to ask?"

Still avoiding the topic, are we?

I nod.

"Truth or dare?" he demands.

"Truth."

"Why did you come to my room that night?"

I consider my answer for a few seconds, then I stare at him boldly and say, "I wanted to hit on you. Or have you hit on me." To stop him from asking more, I press the game forward. "Truth or dare?"

"Truth."

"Why choose someone you don't really like?"

"No risk of getting hurt."

"Also no risk of getting happy. Is that why you always pretend you don't care about anything or anyone? Because the last time you cared, it ended badly?"

Richard looks down. "I guess, sometimes it just feels easier that way. Truth or dare?"

"Truth."

"The morning after, when you shut me out of your room, you were jealous."

It's more of a statement than a question.

I nod. "Truth or dare?"

His eyes darken. "Dare."

I swallow and, never breaking eye contact, I speak two simple life-changing words. "Kiss me."

Slowly, deliberately, Richard closes the space between us. He cups my face and looks at me a moment longer before his lips are on mine and the world tilts upside-down. I lose myself in the kiss. It's gentle at first, tentative, exploring. Then needier, hungry. I want it to never stop, but it does all too quickly.

Richard nuzzles my neck, whispering, "Truth or dare?"

"Dare."

"Stay at my place tonight."

Eighteen

Never Sleep With Someone On The First Date

Outside the bar, I feel dizzy. And it has nothing to do with the alcohol and everything to do with the man walking by my side.

"Want to take the short or long way home?" Richard asks. "Long one has a view."

"Long way it is, I could use some fresh air."

Richard takes my hand and leads the way. The simple gesture makes me ridiculously giddy, especially when his thumb brushes against my palm, making me shiver with the uncontrollable desire to feel those hands all over me.

Halfway between the Brooklyn and Manhattan bridges, we stop and lean against the railing to admire the view. *Breathtaking.*

A pang of jealousy stabs me in the chest. "Is this where you take all your girls?"

Oh, why did I open my stupid mouth? Blair Walker, shut up and don't ruin the moment.

"Actually, no. I usually come here alone."

"Do you?"

"I enjoy the view."

"Yep." I focus on the glittering lights reflected on the water. "Manhattan is irresistible when she's wearing lights."

"I know someone else who's irresistible." Suddenly Richard's voice is behind me, his lips brushing my ear.

I turn to look at him and find myself imprisoned between the railing and his strong chest. The scent of his aftershave is intoxicating, and my hands move of their own accord up the crisp cotton of his shirt. After tracing his thumb around my earlobe with one hand, he moves the other under my chin and tilts my head up. Then we're kissing again, his mouth on mine, gently parting my lips. My hands become frantic, my entire body prickling with anticipation.

I pull away and say, "I think we should go home."

Richard leaves a trail of soft kisses down my neck. "Sorry for making us take the long road." He grabs my hand, and we speed-walk through Brooklyn, leaving Manhattan and her lights behind.

For the entire elevator ride to his loft, we make out like a pair of teenagers: bodies wrapped together, oblivious to anything else in the world. Completely lost in each other.

When the doors ping open, we tumble out and laugh our way to Richard's door. He gets the keys out of his pocket and lets us in.

"Welcome back," Richard whispers.

"Why are we whispering?" I ask in an equally low voice.

"Chevron might be asleep."

"Oh, right. Where is she?"

I tiptoe into the living room to find Chevron sprawled on the couch—belly up, legs in the air. I brace my hands on the backrest, staring at her, but soon get distracted by Richard hugging me from behind and kissing my neck. Shivers spread down my shoulders and along my spine, making my toes curl. I turn around and press my lips onto Richard's.

My body is taking over in a way I've never experienced. This man has melted my brain. My heart is beating so fast I'm afraid I might pass out. But what if this is a huge mistake? Richard is still my boss.

"Are you sure you want this?" I breathe, my ribcage bobbing up and down convulsively.

"Walker"—his teeth find my earlobe—"we reached the point

of no return a while ago."

Yeah, agreed.

Richard bends slightly and swings an arm behind my knees, lifting me up and carrying me to the bedroom.

There, on his bed, we make love. I'm confident we're not just having sex. Yes, it's sensual, and heated… but if he does not say so in words, the way Richard looks at me tells me everything. I've never made love keeping my eyes open, but with Richard, it seems impossible to close them.

***

Joy. Indecent bliss. Never have I ever felt so good in my life. I roll over the bed, only to crash-land on hard muscle.

I blink. "Mmm, I remember this room…"

Richard brushes a strand of hair off my face. "Hope this time you remember why you're here."

Oh, I *so* do. Flashes of last night make me blush.

"I see that you do." Richard grabs my hand and kisses the tips of my fingers.

"I might need a little reminder."

"Careful what you wish for…"

I giggle as Richard throws the blankets away and his lips start their magic again…

In a fog of passion and burning emotions, the rest of the day is spent in bed. We only leave to take Chevron for a *very short* walk. I can't stop smiling and feeling all dreamy and happy and, well… sated.

Saturday night, we attempt to leave Richard's apartment to get some dinner. But it's a stupid mistake. We get seated and we order like two normal people would. But then we start this flirtatious eye game, which evolves in us casually touching each other's arms or legs, until we're kissing—*ahem,* making out in the restaurant like two teenagers. By the time the food arrives, Richard asks for everything to be boxed. He pays the bill and we're back at his house and in bed less than an hour after we left.

***

Sunday evening is when the bubble of happiness bursts. The pin comes in the form of an ominous suggestion from Richard. It happens in the late afternoon while we're drinking tea on the couch, my bare legs in his lap and Chevron lying quietly on the living room rug.

I'm admiring Richard's naked chest—he's wearing only sweatpants—when my fit watch sends me a pulsing notification I've been lying down for too long. A pretty common occurrence in the past two days. Out of habit, I check the time. *Already so late.* I wish I could stay in Richard's apartment wearing only one of his T-shirts forever. But I can't. I drop my empty mug on the coffee table and sigh. "Chevron," I say, patting her head. "Time to go."

"Already?" Richard protests. "It's only five!"

"Yeah, but by the time we get to Manhattan it'll be late, and tomorrow is going to be busy. If you haven't noticed, we made quite a splash Friday."

"Stay longer, I can give you a ride…"

As tempting as the offer is…

"We've been in bed for two days," I say, blushing. "I could use the walk. And you'll see us both tomorrow morning at the office, anyway."

"Speaking of the office." Richard's expression switches from a relaxed smile to a slight frown. "It'd be better if we kept this quiet, at least for now."

A chill runs down my spine. Sure, I'd had the same thought.

Not wanting to have everyone else at work involved in my private life and gossiping seems like a good idea on the surface. But hearing Richard voice the same concern sets off a million alarm bells in my head. Why does he want to keep it quiet? To protect our privacy? To give us time to figure out our feelings before anyone else gets involved? Or would keeping the relationship hidden only make it easier to break off?

I want to reply that it's okay. Tell him I understand. I want to, but find I can't. After almost forty-eight hours spent naked, I'm less lost in a whirlwind of lust and able to pause long enough to question what's happening.

"Why keep it quiet?" I ask.

"It'd be awkward if the others knew about us."

Us. What does that even mean? I know I'm supposed to play cool, not make demands after such a short time. To let things evolve on their own, so as not to scare him away. It's acknowledged dating wisdom. Yet, there's a new fire burning within me that simply won't let me play by the rules.

I fold my legs and sit straighter. "For them, or for you?"

Clinginess taints my voice and I hate myself for it.

"For everyone, including you."

"Come on, Richard. We don't work in that kind of place. Everyone would just be happy for us."

The afterglow vaporizes from his face, replaced by a tense grimace. "Maybe, but what if I'm not ready to share my private life with all my employees?"

"Indira seems to always know who you're dating."

"Yes, but this is different."

"I would certainly hope so."

"What's that supposed to mean?"

"That if you're only looking for another two-week relationship, I'm not interested."

"So what are you interested in?"

"I don't know, why don't you tell me?"

"Calm down. Why are you getting so worked up?"

The answer comes from my twisting guts before I can even form a rational thought. And since I've no gut-to-mouth filters, I yell, "Because I'm in love with you!"

The silence that follows this impromptu declaration is so tense that even Chevron lifts her head to check on us. Richard is staring at me with that deer-in-the-headlights expression. Well, "terrorized to death" wasn't exactly the reaction I was hoping for. Tears prick my eyes and I have to blink fast to hold them back. Still, Richard isn't speaking.

"Don't worry," I say, getting up. "You don't have to say it back."

Coward, *I add in my head.* I know you feel the same.

I can't stand to look at his terrified expression for a second longer, so I dart for the bedroom. I manage to throw on the essentials before Richard comes in. Admittedly, having this argument wearing only a lacy bra and panties is hardly any better.

"What do you want from me?" he asks.

"Guess."

"What, love?" He scoffs. "A wedding proposal? You want the house with the white fence, the three kids, and a dog in the yard?"

"I already have a dog!" I scream. "And what's wrong with wanting any of that? What if my dream is to get married and have a family?"

"Well, that's not my dream."

"Isn't it? Or are you too afraid to admit it is, even to yourself, because your dream already got shattered once."

"This has nothing to do with that... don't throw my past in

my face as an excuse for me not agreeing with your cloud nine attitude."

"Are you sure? Seems to me you hide a lot behind that past."

"You've no idea what you're talking about."

"No, I do. You're the clueless one."

"Oh, really?"

"Yeah, really."

"Why?"

"Because I told you I'm in love with you and you lost the ability to speak."

Richard stands there, gaping. Again, not a word.

I grab my pants and slide them on. "There you go again."

"Blair." He takes a few steps toward me and places one hand on each of my shoulders. "You're overreacting."

"No, Richard." I shove his hands away and grab my blouse. "You're underreacting!"

"Underreacting? What does that even mean?"

Finally dressed, I do a frantic scan of the room to locate all my scattered possessions. I toss everything in the duffel bag and put on my gym shoes. Ready to leave, I turn toward him. "It means that I just told you 'I love you' and I deserve to hear more back than a never ending silence."

Again, silence is all he gives me.

I push past him and storm out of the bedroom. In the living room, I hook Chevron to her leash. Richard hasn't followed me. Oh, no, he prefers to stay hidden. Easier that way. *Bastard. Asshole. Coward.* Tears blur my vision at last. I wait a few more seconds for him to come out. He doesn't. With my heart shattering, I dash out of the apartment, banging the door behind me as hard as I can.

For the entire walk home, I keep looking over my shoulder hoping to see a silver car following us. Every time a car passes us, my heart jolts in my chest. But it's never Richard. I make my way toward Manhattan, sobbing uncontrollably. So much so that a few people stop me to ask if I need help. I turn away the kind strangers, explaining it's only a problem of the heart. *Only.* Why is it that I'm more heartbroken after a two-night stand than I was over a three-year relationship? Is this what love does to you? If that's it, I hope I can fall out of it as quickly as I fell in.

Nineteen

Never Stress Eat

A few hours later, Nikki arrives home to find me in a state of utter misery. I'm on the couch, in my PJs, surrounded by used Kleenex, and eating ice cream.

My best friend takes in the scene and is at my side at once. "What happened to you?" She takes the bowl of ice cream from me to sniff it, and her nostrils flare. "Is this real ice cream?"

I nod.

"Industrial, processed ice cream?"

I nod again.

"No soy?"

I shake my head.

"Dairy?"

Nod.

"Saturated fats?"

I make a wimpy sound.

"Ah." Nikki places the bowl out of reach and drops onto the couch next to me. "I thought you'd spent the weekend with the boss…"

I stare at her with big eyes, trying to transmit telepathically what happened because saying it aloud is too painful.

She catches my vibes at once. "And before the day was over, you asked him where you stood…"

Nod.

"He freaked out."

Nod.

"You went on the defensive and lashed out."

Whimper.

"Richard got mad, too, the argument escalated, you both became petty, hurt each other as much as you could until you stormed out of his house, banging the door behind you. How am I doing?"

I drop my face into my hands and shake my head.

"*Awhooo,*" Chevron comments.

Nikki sighs. "And all this in front of the dog?"

Face still hidden, I nod.

"The poor thing is traumatized."

I give her a look of desperation.

"Come on," Nikki pulls me into a hug. "Everything will be all right."

"How?"

"You two just have to talk."

I snort. "Yeah, because Richard is so good at expressing his feelings."

"Give him time. You ambushed him when he wasn't ready. You should've let him get more used to you."

"I know I was supposed to wait. But what if I don't want to? What if I want to tell him how I feel when I feel it? Why is that so wrong?"

"Nothing's wrong. But it's wrong to expect Richard to be on the same page right away. Give him some time."

"Oh, he has all the time in the world."

"Meaning?"

"I'm not taking another step toward him. Not one."

"So you're just going to pretend the past forty-eight hours didn't happen?"

"Exactly. If Richard changes his mind, he knows where to find me."

***

Monday morning, I put on a brave face and go to the office. I wear a simple blouse, black capris, and sneakers to be switched with wedges in Brooklyn. *Because Richard doesn't like wedges.* I don't want to spark any extra tension, sexual or otherwise. I just want to get through the day, ignore him, and be ignored back.

I sit at my desk, bend my head low, and will myself to stare at my screen and just my screen. I don't even blink when Richard walks in. He supplies a generic, "Hello," that leaves me free enough not to reply, and then moves on to his office without a second glance in my direction. At least from what I can tell using only my peripheral vision.

So he's going for an avoidance strategy, too. *Very well!* I am the queen of avoidance, I can keep my silent treatment going for weeks if I want to.

> Mon, June 12 at 8:37 AM
>
> @PinkPanther has logged in
>
> R u mad at the boss?

I guess not everyone is willing to ignore me though.

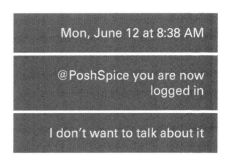

> Mon, June 12 at 8:38 AM
>
> @PoshSpice you are now logged in
>
> I don't want to talk about it

I HAVE NEVER

We're not talking

Okay

I don't want to talk

Write

Or even think about it

???

Leave it alone

No can do

Please let it go

I might start crying

And I'd really rather not

Oh!

Yeah, oh!

You slept together

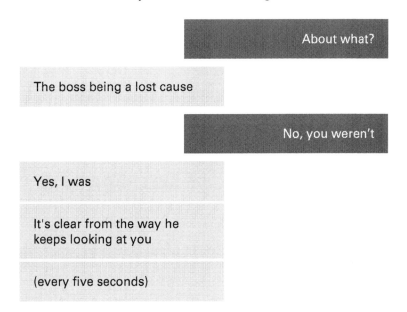

I'm logging off

I was wrong

And she's successfully baited me into asking...

About what?

The boss being a lost cause

No, you weren't

Yes, I was

It's clear from the way he keeps looking at you

(every five seconds)

A dart hits my heart. *Hope? Fear? Love?* All three? I don't know. But I don't have the luxury of indulging in false expectations. Richard has made it clear where he stands. His fear comes before his feelings and that's not going to change no matter what I do.

He's probably just mad

We had a big argument

That's not the face of a "mad man"

Even if he could pass for a younger Jon Hamm

Not in the mood for jokes

I wasn't joking

The boss isn't mad

What is he then?

Terrified

That he is for sure.

And how's that better?

He's terrified because he cares

Doesn't matter if he doesn't care

Or if he's terrified he does care

The bottom line stays the same

We aren't happening

Give it time

He'll come around

Have you read the column?

No

Read the column

Whatever

Don't you have any work to do?

All right Miss Crabby McCranky...

Talk to you later

Mon, June 12 at 9:26 AM

@PinkPanther has logged off

I log off for real this time. It took all my willpower not to open that damn column over breakfast this morning, and now Indira is making my resolve crumble. *I can read a column.* It wouldn't be like talking to him. It's only words on the screen. I mean, what harm could come from it? Before I second-guess myself, I click on the magazine's homepage and open the column.

Someone Once Told Me
by Richard Stratton

> Last night I couldn't rest. Unable to sit still in my apartment with only my thoughts as companions, I went for a walk... and I met Sally.

Sally? Another woman? A sharp pain in my chest makes me swallow as my mouth goes dry with fear. I grab my water bottle and chug a good half before I can bring my eyes back to the screen.

> No, my name is not Harry, and this isn't a romantic story.

Utter relief.

> Sally is a woman in her late fifties, who has been living on the streets of Brooklyn for the better part of ten years, and who could easily pass for a seventy–year–old with her white hair and weathered features.

> On a regular day, I would've passed Sally without even noticing her.

Not last night.

Someone once told me how easily homeless people disappear in the eyes of passers–by, almost becoming invisible. And how surprised I'd be if I stopped for a minute to hear the stories these people have to share.

So I stopped.

I asked Sally what her favorite sandwich was and what she wanted to drink. I bought a meal for both of us and we ate it together sitting on a bench in the park.

And Sally told me her story...

Not one of drugs or alcohol abuse, abandonment, or delinquency. Simply the story of a business investment gone terribly wrong, and Sally's inability to get back on her feet after she lost everything.

I keep reading the details of how Sally invested all her money in a business that ran profitably for fifteen years before she had to file for bankruptcy, losing not only the business but everything else she had, too. But it is the conclusion of the article that gives me pause.

Sally told me all this, not with an air of bitter regret, but with sweet nostalgia in her voice. And when I asked her if she'd change any of her past choices, she told me that no,

she wouldn't. She had followed her dream.
Sally had bet everything she had and lost.
But she'd do it all again, as those years had
been the best of her life...

Richard ends the article with a question.

Would you risk everything you have for a
dream?

I don't know, Richard, *would you?* Seems clear the answer is
still no. Is he comparing me to Sally's business? Saying love
will give temporary ecstasy followed by an inevitable hard
crash? Why did Indira make me read this? I'm the "someone
who once told him," but she can't know that. So what's the
message here? My brain and heart are too exhausted for
guesswork. Sorry, Richard. If you want to tell me something,
you'll have to say it to my face.

After reading the enigmatic column, I spend the rest of the
day battling my instincts. All I want to do is look Richard's way,
but instead, I force my gaze ahead, not straying once.

***

There's an art in avoiding people. In the next few days, I perfect
mine. I time everything so I'll never risk crossing paths with
Richard. Step one, arrive at the office before him and never
leave last. Step two, wait for him to come back from his lunch
break before I take mine. Step three, whatever else Richard
does, make sure I'm always one step ahead or behind so we
never bump into one another.

Wednesday night, dead tired after three days of sitting on
needles, I'm slouched on the couch when my phone rings,

"Umbrella Corporation HR" appearing on the screen. *Yeah, I've renamed Évoque after the zombie-apocalypse-causing corporation in Resident Evil!* What do they want? *Aha!* They realized their mistake and want me back.

My exile in Brooklyn is over!

"Are you going to pick that up or you're just going to let it ring?" Nikki asks from the other end of the couch.

Oh, I'm so picking up. *"Blair Walker."*

"Blair, good evening, this is Natalie Rivers speaking. I'm Emilia Peterson's executive assistant."

"Of course, Natalie. How are you?"

"I'm well, thanks. You?"

"Same here." Pleasantries over, I cut to the chase. "What can I do for you?"

"We recently had an opening for the position of Junior Fashion Editor and we wanted to see if you'd be interested in coming in for an interview."

"Oh, I thought there weren't going to be new openings for a while…"

"Yeah, um…" Natalie sounds embarrassed. "We had a person resign and so the position is open now."

"Is this 'someone' Aurora Vanderbilt?"

"Yes, she quit after… well, I'm sure you know."

I wonder if Aurora really quit or if they gave her a choice between resigning and being fired. Now the tax evasion scandal is out in the open, Évoque will do everything they can to distance the magazine from Maison Vanderbilt. Guess their money is no longer good now that everyone knows where it comes from.

What a bunch of hypocrites.

"Anyway," Natalie continues. "Emilia has an opening in her calendar Friday morning at eight, would that work for you?"

"I'd need to take time off work. Would it be possible to have an appointment in the late evening?"

"I'm sorry, Emilia's very busy. This is her only opening."

That presumptuous bitch. She's asking me to come in for an interview, but of course, I have to adjust my schedule to hers. She knows I want the job more than she wants to give it to me. As much as I can't stand her, this is a real job, at a top magazine. My dream. No matter if I can't stand the HR Manager, it's not like I'll have to work with her. I only need to survive the interview. *Yeah, and go back to work at bitchland, leaving all the nice colleagues, work independence, and the boss you're in love with behind.*

Stop it, Richard won't factor in this decision. Period.

"Okay, Natalie. I'll adjust my schedule. See you on Friday."

Twenty

Never Mix Business and Pleasure

On Thursday night, I don't have the guts to ask Richard in person for a free morning. Not only because we're not on speaking terms, but also because if he were to ask *why,* what would I say? I was never good at lying, and telling the boss about the interview would only be pouring gasoline on the fire. Plus, I don't even know if I'll have anything to tell. This is a preliminary chat. No need to cause a storm yet. I text him at the last minute Friday morning, saying I have a personal matter to attend to, and that I'll be coming in later in the day.

The second hard part is leaving Chevron behind. She's at my feet wagging her tail, ready for our morning walk, but I can't bring a dog to the interview. Still unaware, said pup sits in the hallway, waiting for me to hook her leash.

"Not today, honey."

Chevron's tail slows down.

I open the door. "I'll be back in a couple of hours."

She drops to the floor, tail static, eyes wide. My heart breaks a little as I lock the apartment, leaving her all alone.

What will I do if I accept the new job? I'm sure Évoque doesn't have a bring-your-pet-to-the-office policy. Imagine Chevron running loose in the fashion closet. That would be something. *With a better paycheck, you'll be able to afford the best dog-sitter in the city.* Yeah, Northwestern must know they have to offer me a salary bump for me to even consider going back.

Foldable flats on, I reach Canal Street Station. As I push my way through the ticket barrier, the aboveground spring breeze turns into stale, deep-fried air. Okay, maybe Manhattan's air isn't exactly wholesome. But the underground air is ten times worse. Warm and clingy.

Someone stomps on my foot—not fun when my only protection is foldable flats.

"Hey," I call after the brute.

But the suit ignores me and hurries toward his track. *You sorry excuse for a commuter.* I forgot how rude, pushy, and inconsiderate of other people's existence subway-takers can be. So much better to walk to work. *Easy to say in summer. Wait until it rains, snows, and blizzards, then see how fun it is to walk on a bridge exposed to the elements.*

I squish myself onto the first uptown train and, oh, the stench. Exposed to the elements sounds more promising than squeezed to within an inch of my life by smelly strangers. I'm walled in by three people. If there's one place where being short is a clear disadvantage, it's inside a subway car. Behind me stands an overweight gentleman whose bulging belly is warmly pressed against my back. On my left, a tall girl—I hate genetics right now—has a bony elbow dangerously close to my jaw. And I can count the pills on the tie of the guy standing directly in front of me, who, besides having a dreadful fashion sense, is also drinking coffee from a paper cup.

I watch in horror as Mr. Old Tie removes the plastic lid. Is he *crazy?* The last thing I need is a hot-coffee shower. I try to edge back. But bulgy-guy's belly stops me. I search left and right for an escape route. Nothing. My head is level with my fellow riders' shoulders at best; I can't see anything. I can't breathe. Please, New York fairies, let this ride be a short one.

I spend the next thirty minutes watching that paper cup like a hawk. When I finally emerge on Columbus Circle, unharmed, if not a bit traumatized, I take a few deep breaths of air, even relishing the smog. If I come back to work at Northwestern, I'll walk. I'll get Chevron a dog-sitter nearby. *What about winter?* She'll get a doggy rainbreaker, I don't care. I'm never taking that line at seven in the morning ever again. If my relationship with Gerard had one merit, it was his Park Avenue address.

I swap flats for stiletto heels and cross the threshold of Northwestern's evil tower of power. The glass and steel are overwhelmingly cold around me. *Oh, so now you even miss brick walls and decrepit wooden floors?* What if I do? *Just saying, you used to love the power of glass and stainless steel.* Right, used to. Before they kicked me to the curb. *So what are you doing here?* It's business. A publishing house wants to make me an offer and I want to hear it. Mini-mental-me snickers at that.

As I did the first time I ever set foot in the building, I have to register as a guest at the reception desk. It feels weird not to bypass security. The receptionist hands me a visitor pass and starts giving me directions to Emilia's office. Great, my least favorite place in the building.

"I know where Ms. Peterson's office is, thanks." I cut the girl short and make my way upstairs.

Emilia's office is the same: white everything and minimalist. Emilia also appears the same paper thin and groomed within an inch of her life. She invites me to sit with the warmth of a popsicle. I take my place on the white chair opposite her white desk and fold my hands on the immaculate surface.

Emilia's icy blue eyes follow the gesture with an air of disgust. Is she worried I'll taint her space? Is she a germ freak? Her eyes focus an extra second on the tip of my fingers and her nose creases in the slightest wrinkle.

I quickly pull my hands down and check my nails. My index is missing a microscopic speckle of nail polish. So, yeah. I stopped doing my nails every night and started doing them every other night—or two. *Big deal!*

Emilia's displeased scrutiny continues. This time, I follow her razor-sharp gaze to my blouse where, just over my left breast, there's a tiny—again, almost-invisible-to-the-naked-eye—brown circle. So a droplet of that man's coffee *did* land on me. Oh, well. *Shoot me.* It's not like I'm wearing a T-shirt that says Cece Chanol.

How could I forget how much pressure they put on appearances here? A few months in Brooklyn have relaxed my standards to unacceptable levels of shabbiness it seems, given the sour expression on Emilia's face. What a wonderful way to start the interview. Was Emilia forced to offer me the job despite her—almost certain—recommendation against it?

"So, Blair. How have you been?"

"Great, thank you." *But no thanks to you.* "You?"

"Busy, as always."

I think she meant, "Bitchy, as always."

Emilia continues. "Tell me about your experience at this"—she stares at my CV and raises an eyebrow—"online *hub* you've been working at."

I launch into a professional presentation of my achievements over the last few months. The regular beauty features I've established. The team of influencers I've put together. The sponsorships. The celebrity photoshoots and interviews... The more I talk, the more I surprise even myself at the amount of work I accomplished in such a short time. I basically built an entire fashion magazine from scratch. An awesome one.

Emilia lets me talk, her face a studiously unimpressed one. "That all sounds marvelous," she comments when I'm finished. "Now, as I'm sure you remember, here at Évoque we operate on a high-end profile. As a Junior Editor, you'll only be in charge of assisting more competent and experienced professionals."

"So I wouldn't be responsible for any project? Not even smaller features?"

"Never say never. We're very open minded and it's our desire to groom the next generation of leaders. So we encourage all employees to bring forward new ideas…"

Her rehearsed speech is dribbling with so much condescension, I can't listen. I'm finally back on the thirty-eighth floor of this shiny Manhattan skyscraper, and I can't seem to find a single good reason to be here and work with these people. *It's your dream, always has been.* Yeah, but why? Why was it ever my dream to work at Évoque? Why come back? This company used me for years and then discarded me without a second thought. And all they're offering now is another junior position with no real independence. *One you would've killed for a short while ago.* Only because I didn't know better.

"So you encourage the people who work here to bring forward new ideas?" I challenge her.

"Of course, we do."

"You mean like when the story about Maison Vanderbilt committing tax fraud was brought forward."

Emilia's nostrils flare. "Blair, in case you've forgotten we're a fashion magazine, we don't do investigative journalism. Now, I'm sure at this"—she waves one hand in the air dismissively—"online-whatever you've been working for, lines and roles were more… let's say blurred, but—"

"Of the fifty-or-so papers under the umbrella of Northwestern Publishing, not a single one could've picked up the story?"

"I honestly don't see what you're trying to accomplish with this sterile polemic."

"I'm trying to say that this company doesn't encourage

people to bring forward ideas, it forces them to kill stories to keep easy advertising money flowing in."

"Blair, let me be perfectly clear. This is a unique opportunity. You blew your first chance at a serious career and were lucky enough to get a second, which doesn't happen very often and wasn't the wisest idea in the first place if you ask me... You won't get a third."

Oh, she's just confirmed my worst fears. Someone higher up forced Emilia's hand, but she never wanted to offer me the job. The Talent Manager Coordinator hates me. Which means she'd try to make my head roll every chance she got. Another good reason *not to* come back.

I stand up. "No, Emilia. *I'd* like to be perfectly clear. *You* screwed up *your* first chance by promoting the wrong person for the wrong reasons. This was your second chance, and *you* blew it. Sorry, you won't get a third. Goodbye."

I don't wait for a reply, I simply show myself out of the witch's office. *Humph, goodbye.* There should be a better word. I don't want to wish her *good*bye, I want to say *bad*-bye. In the long elevator ride down, I envision a whole article on the topic.

Title: The Power of Bad-Bye
Subtitle: When Enough Is Enough

In the lobby, I give back my pass, hardly paying attention, already typing the first paragraph of the article in my head. With no regrets, I walk out of Évoque for the last time.

***

That afternoon I knock on Richard's door as soon as I get into the office.

Richard lifts his eyes from a document, and a deep frown

appears as he spots me standing behind the glass. He waves me in with a dismissive flick of his fingers.

Uh-oh.

This is the first time I've approached him since our fight on Sunday and he gives me attitude? I thought we could defuse the situation and at least try to be civil to each other. After this morning, I have a deeper appreciation of the trust Richard has put in me. Sadly, only professionally. I've also realized I love the work I'm doing here and that I want to keep doing it regardless of my personal feelings for the boss. But if he wants to give me attitude, I can give attitude right back.

"What do you want?" Richard fires at me.

"Hello, good afternoon to you, too," I snap back.

"Yeah, exactly. *After*noon. Glad you finally decided to show up."

"I texted you to say I needed the morning off."

He pierces me with an angry look. "And why was that?"

I stare at him, frozen.

Does he know about the job interview? How could he?

I'm still not talking, so Richard scoffs. "That's what I thought."

We glare at each other for a few more seconds before he adds, "Are you handing in your notice?"

He knows. "No, I'm not. Yeah, I went to an interview, but I didn't accept the offer." That seems to throw him a little. "So you can take your self-righteousness and stick it... well, I'm sure I don't need to tell you where."

"The great Blair Walker will be staying with us another day. How exciting."

"What's that supposed to mean? I just told you I didn't take the job. Why do you have to be a dick about it?"

"Because since the first day you signed your contract, you've been waiting for the moment you could get out."

"That's not true. I've busted my ass off to create something from nothing for this magazine and I've given it one-hundred percent. You can't deny that. And, yes, Northwestern offered me a job at a magazine with a better name, better pay, and better benefits. So I went and listened to what they had to say. Shoot me." I raise my hands in surrender. "But I turned the offer down because I believe in what we're building."

My volume has gone up a notch and I'm uncomfortably aware that everyone outside must be able to hear us. If our body language wasn't already clear enough. *Stupid glass walls!*

"If you say so."

Richard's dismissive attitude sparks more anger and frustration. He wants to pretend nothing has happened between us? He wants to ignore his feelings? I've let him so far, but now he's pushed all the wrong buttons and I'm furious enough to tackle the real problem between us.

"Are you mad at me for the job offer, or are you mad at yourself because you can't admit what's really bothering you?"

"And what would that be?" Richard sneers.

"That you got scared you'd lose me for good, and you're too afraid to admit you have feelings for me."

"That's a bit presumptuous on your part."

"Then tell me it isn't true! Tell me I'm wrong. I mean, if you're not too afraid."

"Careful, Walker. You're taking it too far."

"You can puff out your chest all you like, the fact remains you're too much of a coward to admit the truth."

Richard jumps up from his chair. "Who are you calling a coward?"

"You, it's what you are!"

"It's better if we end this conversation now before either of us says something we can't take back. You want the truth: I can't stand to look at you right now."

"Oh, the coward wants to run away. How surprising."

"I'm out of here." Richard rounds his desk and is out of the door and leaving the main office before I can say anything.

Nuh-uh. He's so not getting out of this one.

I follow him. "You want to run?" I yell. "*Fine.* Run! But remember I can run faster."

I don't care if everyone in the office is blatantly staring at us. It's time Richard and I had this discussion and if he wants to have it in full public... *his choice.*

He stops in his track and turns toward me, eyes glaring. "What's that even supposed to mean?"

"That I don't quit. That I don't run away from the things that scare me. I run *after* what I want."

"No, you live in a world of unicorns and rainbows. Real life is not like that."

"Real life is what you make of it."

"Walker, I'm sorry. I don't live in a pink cloud of optimism."

"No, right. You prefer a black hole of fear." *Ah, gotcha.* He gapes at me but doesn't reply so I go ahead and announce it to the world, "I love you, Richard Stratton, and I'm not afraid of saying it."

"Love isn't enough."

"Love is everything."

"It's not."

"It is for me. Tell me you don't love me and you're free to go. This is the last you'll hear of it. Come on, say it. SAY IT!"

Frown deeper than ever, jaw clenched, Richard shakes his head. With a seething look, he turns on his heel and walks out of the office.

Bang! The doors slam shut, and I'm left standing in the

middle of the room like an idiot. Chest heaving, breath ragged, the same as if I had just run a marathon.

I lost.

People around me seem intent on their screens. They must think I'm a t-Rex. That if they don't move, I won't know they exist. Even Indira is avoiding my gaze. *Figures.* What could they possibly say to a colleague who just embarrassed herself in the worst possible way and was publicly turned down by her boss, *their* boss?

The only soul who shows any sympathy is Chevron. She nuzzles my calves in a comforting gesture, whining understandingly.

What now? Should I crawl back to Manhattan and beg Évoque for the job? It's clear I can't keep working here. I knew having a relationship with the boss was wrong. I knew commitment-phobic men don't turn into commitment-happy boyfriends overnight. Despite all that, I gave it my best try, and now I'm back where I started. No job. No love life. Well, at least I have a loyal companion. I pat Chevron's head, pick my dignity up off the floor, and turn back toward my desk. I need to collect my things and get ready to leave. For the day? Forever? I don't know.

That's when the office door bursts open again and there's a collective gasp. Indira lifts her eyes from the screen, her expression changing from I'm-so-busy-pretending-you-don't-exist to well-well-well-let's-see-what-happens-now.

Very slowly, I turn and watch Richard storm back into the room.

Twenty-one

Never Wash Dirty Laundry in Public

"I can't tell you that," Richard says without preamble.

Storm and thunder are dancing in his brown irises, now almost black. The face I love so much is set in a look of determined anger, ferociously handsome and just plain fierce at the same time. Something lurches inside me and my throat constricts.

Richard shakes his head as if trying to sort conflicting thoughts. "I promised I wouldn't be here, ever again."

I drop the duffel bag and take a step forward. "Where's here?"

Richard looks up again, his eyes wide, vulnerable, without a trace of cynicism—and as they meet mine, the world stops. That one look tells me more than a thousand words could; Richard's expression tells me he loves me. But I can't be the only one acknowledging her feelings. So I ask again, "Where's here?"

"Here is where I'm about to make a fool of myself, *again.*"

"Why?"

"Because I do love you."

Tears of relief spring to my eyes.

"There's nothing foolish about that."

"No?" He lets out a hysterical laugh. "Love has only ever brought me pain and humiliation. I tried to avoid it, suppress it, deny it." Richard rubs his forehead and I wait patiently in silence. "But the burning just won't go away. And I've never been more scared in my life. For years, I've managed just fine on my own. But then, no, you had to come along and ruin everything. So *here* is where my heart is again in the hands of a woman who can do whatever the hell she wants with it."

"Richard, I'm not your ex."

"No, you're not."

"You say that as if it's a bad thing."

"Because it is."

"Why?"

A painful grimace twists his features. "Because I never loved her the way I love you!" The heart that was hammering in my chest until a few seconds ago stops. "Since you left on Sunday, I haven't been able to sleep, eat, work, think. You're everywhere. I can't stop thinking about you. Even if you refused to talk to me, I couldn't wait to get to the office every day to see you, and I dread the time of day when I have to go home alone. Then when you didn't show up today, I thought you were leaving, for good."

"But I wasn't."

"This time or ever?"

"Are we talking about a job here or something else?"

"We're not talking about a bloody job."

"Richard." I take another step forward. "I can't promise everything will be perfect, that we'll never argue or break up. And I don't know if we'll have a happily ever after. But I'm willing to risk my heart on that possibility. I'm in… one hundred percent."

"What if I don't want to get married?"

"I don't want to marry you." Okay, I might've doodled Blair Stratton more than once, but that doesn't mean anything. "You haven't even taken me on a real date yet."

Someone in the background cheers. It could be Indira. Or Saffron. Or even Chevron for all I know.

"What if I don't want to get married, *ever?*" Richard insists.

I sigh. "Do I want to get married at some point in my life? *Yes.* Would I consider not doing it for the right man? Seems so. I always thought I wanted a wedding. But I also wanted many other things that I've discovered were insignificant. So is a piece of paper more important than the real love of a real man? No. I watched my mother spend years in a marriage with no love. She stood by a man she didn't love, but wouldn't leave only to be proper. And that's not what I want. If marriage is the one thing you can't give me, I'd rather not have it and have everything else."

"You say that now, but you'll change your mind."

"Maybe I will, maybe I won't. Maybe you'll change your mind." He's about to protest, but I anticipate him. "Let me finish. I spent my whole life mapping out every single step I should take. Engaged by twenty-nine, married by thirty, and two point five kids by thirty-five. Same goes for my career. Then my perfect plan crumbled in a single day. I lost the perfect job and the perfect-on-paper boyfriend and I've never been happier. I don't want to plan anymore, I want to live."

"What if it doesn't work?"

"What if it does? Can you walk away without trying? 'Cause I sure can't."

"If we do this…" This time, it's Richard taking a step toward me. "What is the single thing you'd never give me?"

I take a moment to think. "My career," I say. "I'll never be a stay-at-home mom."

Richard's features relax for the first time since our conversation started, and he closes the distance between us. I inhale his scent and I'm a goner as soon as he cups my face in his hands. "So we're having kids now?" he asks with a playful smile.

I blush and luckily don't have the time to stutter an embarrassing reply as Richard's lips silence mine. His strong arms wrap around me and he almost crushes me against his chest.

I'm pretty sure kissing the boss in the middle of the office is against every workplace protocol ever written. But right now, I'm too busy trying to stand on my own two legs to care. That thing they say about buckling knees? *Totally true.*

We finally let go, and Richard seems to become aware of the gaping faces staring at us from all around the office. Ada is clapping and crying, too, I think. I can't tell under her giant cat-eye glasses. Indira is sporting a shrewd smile. Saffron is taking a pic. Surely she doesn't plan to post it on the magazine's socials, right? And the boys are trying to project a look of composed appreciation.

"Come on, kids," Indira yells, breaking the tension of the

moment. "Cheer up for mommy and daddy, they made up."

Everyone laughs and claps and cheers. And I'm so stupidly happy I can't talk. I can only keep smiling at the man I love, whose eyes now reflect the same love he must see in mine.

"What happens now?" I whisper.

My anger has burned out and I'm becoming very self-conscious. Shouting my feelings in front of all my colleagues and forcing a love admission out of Richard were not part of the plan when I woke up this morning.

"We can start with a first date," Richard says. "Dinner?"

"It's two-thirty, I'm not hungry."

Richard leans in and whispers, "Oh, you will be. Because we're stopping at my place first."

I blush a furious red and hide my face in Richard's chest.

"Everyone," Richard says aloud. "It's been a long week. Let's take the rest of the day off."

The cheers that follow this announcement are even more widespread and enthusiastic.

Richard takes my hand and whistles for Chevron to follow us out of the office. As we reach the door and exit, an echo of Indira's comment reaches me. "... if they'd told me all it took to have the afternoon off was to get the boss laid, I would've pimped him more."

"Indira." Ada's voice is barely audible through the door. "You've missed the whole point. It's not about getting laid, it's about love."

"Please don't tell me we have another hopeless romantic in the house..."

Mercifully, the elevator arrives and I can't hear any more of Indira's pretend-cynic comments.

The three of us step in, and as soon as the doors swipe closed, Richard pushes me into a corner. One hand on my lower back, the other buried in my hair.

"I love you." He nibbles my earlobe. "It's so good to say it. I love you."

"I love you, too," I whisper, trying not to combust.

"*Woof, woof.*" Chevron joins the party at our feet, yapping happily.

We pull apart and scratch her behind both ears.

"Yes, we love you, too," I say.

Richard squeezes my hand and I stare into his eyes, realizing I don't care if he's never going to propose. Our trio feels more like a family than anything I've ever had before.

Twenty-two

Don't Move In Without a Ring

Six months later...

Stretching in bed has become difficult. With Chevron—now grown into a medium-sized dog—sprawled over my feet and Richard on my right side, even my tiny figure is experiencing space rationing. Regardless of Richard's California King Bed. But the cozy warmth of two bodies pressed against mine is particularly delicious on a cold winter day.

Outside Richard's window, a rainstorm is attacking New York. It's been pouring since Monday, meaning I've spent three nights in a row at Richard's place. The boyfriend doesn't seem upset about it, but sometimes I suspect that even if he were, he'd be too British to tell me.

Rain or no rain, I have to give him a night's respite and I need a change of clothes, anyway. At five thirty, a vibrating wrist tells me it's time to get out of bed. Richard's building has a gym in the basement, meaning I can run despite the weather. But also that, even stuffing my duffel bag to the brim, between training gear, PJs, bathroom stuff, and day clothes, three days is the max autonomy I have without going back home.

Once training is over, I take Chevron out to relieve herself. When I get back into the apartment, I'm soaked, muddy, and miserable. *I hate the rain.* Before it started, the city was covered in a coat of fluffy white snow; it was a winter wonderland. But now it has all melted into a gloomy puddle.

After a very long shower, I change into my last spare outfit and kiss Richard awake, kick-starting our morning ritual. Richard prepares the oatmeal while I set a pot of water to warm for the French press. Considering the world outside is the saddest gray, Richard surprises me by staring at the storm with a contented smile.

I measure the coffee beans and put them in the grinder. When the noise is over I say, "You seem awfully happy about the bad weather."

Richard shrugs, adding a delicious mix of nuts and fresh fruit to our oatmeal. The boyfriend still eats meat, but he's being surprisingly open-minded about my dietary habits.

"At least one of us is excited about the rain." I pour the heated water and ground coffee into the press, stir, and set the microwave timer to five minutes. "Can you drive us to Manhattan tonight?"

"Tired of Brooklyn?"

"No, but it's been raining for three days... I've run out of clean clothes." I sit at the kitchen bar opposite Richard. "I need to go home and pick up some fresh outfits."

Richard smiles a goofy smile. "I'll let you in on a secret. There's a mystical object with the magical power of turning dirty clothes into clean ones. It's called a washing machine."

I chuckle. "Most of my things are dry-clean."

"There are dry cleaners in Brooklyn."

"Yeah, I'm aware. I'd still prefer to go home and get a fresh change. Come on, I can't show up at work with the same outfit two times in a week."

"Why don't you bring some of your stuff here?"

"Nah, I wouldn't want my wardrobe spread around two places. I'd get confused about where everything is."

Richard seems disappointed by my answer, but the timer interrupts him before he can express his mind. I plunge the press, pour the coffee, and we eat in silence. The mood has shifted from cozy-homey to awkward, and I don't know what I did wrong.

Surely, Richard isn't touchy over my choice of dry cleaners, and I was positive he'd be eager for an evening on his own.

Two spoonfuls of oatmeal, and Richard stops midway through the third to not-so-casually say, "So move everything here."

I choke on a sip of coffee. "Move in with you?"

Whoa! I thought I'd have to rope the boyfriend into this new commitment *very slowly*. And now he's just asking me out of the blue over breakfast on a Thursday in December.

"I mean." His lips twitch. "If you can stomach the idea of living in Brooklyn."

"It's not that. It's just... are you sure?"

"I am, but you don't seem too excited."

"No, I am. But I don't want you to rush into a commitment that might be too quick and backfire on us."

"Think this is rushed? I'll give you rushed." Richard sits taller on his stool. "With my ex, I proposed after six months and pushed her to set the wedding date in another six months without having spent a single day under the same roof."

Richard never talks about his past so I listen without interrupting.

"I sensed she wasn't ready, but I pressed on. Thought that if I didn't give her time to overanalyze, she'd be fine. Well, you know how that ended. That was rushed. This"—he swings his spoon between us, wielding it like a sword—"isn't rushed. You're not pressing me into anything. I'm asking you."

"Okay." I still feel like I'm walking on eggshells. "Take some extra time to mull it over. Then, if you're still sure..."

"I don't need extra time."

I'm at a loss for words... I so didn't expect this.

"You want to know why I'm happy it's raining?" Richard continues.

Oh, so he *was* pleased by the awful weather. I nod.

"Rain means you spend the night. A sunny day means you go back to your place, and I'm alone. I hate sunny days."

"You hate the sun because of me?"

"Despise it."

A dumb smile appears on my lips. "Ah well, in that case…"

"Should I free a drawer?"

"Poor man. You've no idea what you just got yourself into. I'm going to need much more space than a drawer." My brain whizzes with all the technical, organizational steps. "I'd need to give Nikki some notice. I can't just stop paying my share of the rent and leave her out to hang. Plus, she hates the holidays, but…" I get up, another thought suddenly bolting through my head. "Wait here."

I retrieve my bag from down the hall and fish inside for something I haven't looked at in months. After some rummaging, I remember it's in my wallet. A piece of paper so crumpled and frail it might disintegrate at any second.

"What's that?" Richard asks.

Spreading the sheet on the bar, I ask, "You don't recognize it?"

"Is it the list?"

"Mmm-hmm. And there's just one item in there I haven't ticked off yet."

"Which is?"

"Don't move in without a ring."

"Oh, I never considered that angle. Does it bother you?"

"I always thought I wanted to be super traditional, but that was the old me."

Richard is still staring at the list, frowning now. "And when did you go skinny dipping, exactly?"

I blush and snatch the paper away. "I'm never telling you that."

"Hey." Richard makes to grab the sheet again.

I yank my arm away, crumple the list into a ball, and throw it across the hall. Richard doesn't need to re-read every insignificant item. Chevron woofs and runs after the paper ball. After catching it, she sits quietly in a corner, the ball between her front paws, chewing bits away. As I watch the poor piece of paper being shredded to confetti, I realize that the list, however wrong it was in principle, did come through for me in the end. Only not in the way I expected. With every item ticked off in reverse, life has never been better. Magical, spontaneous, and totally unplanned.

"That was naughty," Richard protests.

I round the bar and plant myself between Richard's legs, wrapping my arms around his neck. "You still in the market for a naughty roommate?"

Richard pulls me closer by the waist. "You don't care that it's Brooklyn?"

"I wouldn't care if it were New Jersey with you."

We both know I'm lying, but I quickly silence his rebuff with a kiss.

Mid-kiss, Richard tickles my sides. "When did you go skinny dipping?"

"Aaah, stop. *Stop!*" I struggle to get away. "I'm not talking."

"Yes, you are."

I wriggle free and make a dash for the bedroom.

"Gotcha." Richard pins me on the bed and starts the tickling torture again.

With him on top of me, my giggles soon die away, cutting off completely as his hands start moving in a different way on my body.

I smirk. "You're the worst interrogator ever."

"Being in love with the victim doesn't help, I guess."

"Shut up and kiss me, roommate."

Note from the Author

Dear Reader,

Thanks so much for coming back to the series, it means a lot that you decided to stick with me, and I hope you enjoyed *I Have Never* just as much as you did *Love Connection*. If you haven't read the first book in the series, you can catch up with the story of how Richard got his heart broken in London.

The next story in the *First Comes Love* series will follow Nikki's search for love, and I'm super excited to say it'll be a Christmas story. And in case you were wondering about that gorgeous Hollywood actor, a future book in the series will see the return of Christian Slade with a storyline set in LA.

Now I have to ask you a huge favor. Whether you loved or hated *I Have Never,* please consider leaving a review on the retailer website where you purchased the book and/or Goodreads. Reviews are the biggest gift you can give to an author, and word-of-mouth is the most powerful means of book discovery.

Thank you for your support!

Love,
Camilla

Acknowledgments

First, as always, I'd like to thank you for reading this book and for making my work meaningful.

A special thanks goes to my online family: book bloggers, the book-loving community, and my Street Team. Thank you all for your help and constant support. And in particular, thank you to fellow author and book blogger Aimee Brown for organizing the amazing blog tour for *I Have Never*.

Many thanks to my two editors, Hayley Stone and Helen Baggott.

Thank you to my beta-readers Aimee, Desi, and Lily.

Cover images credits: Designed by Freepik.com
Cover images credits: Designed by Vexels.com

Printed in Great Britain
by Amazon